Illuminations of My Soul

Ravenwolf

First Printing: 2021

Hyperbole Publishing
www.houseofravenwolf.com

Contents

4

My Wish for You

My wish for you is that you find your joy in whatever you seek.

May your dreams stay big, your worries stay small and your thoughts always stay happy.

My wish for you is that you always find your way and discover the things that stir your soul and awaken your heart.

May you always see the best in everyone, choose to always be kind and fall in love with being alive every day.

My wish for you is that you'll always have your face to the sunlight and the wind at your back, sailing as far and wide as your hopes and dreams will carry you.

May you always uncover the magic in your life and stardust in your soul.

My wish is that you'll always remember you're loved, you're special and you're truly one of a kind.

May you always remember that dreams do come true and love never fails.

May your uniqueness always shine through and your passion lift you up.

With a courage that never fails, character that never falters and a heart that never quits, may you always be a light wherever you go.

I wish all these things for you today and all other days, so that you will always celebrate happiness and see the wonder all around you.

Most of all, I wish you love as I celebrate you and all that you mean to me:

You make life that much brighter, feelings that much more alive,
dreams just a little bit more vivid and love that much more beautiful.
That, Darlin', is and always will be …
my wish for you.

Choose to Be the Lady Who Removes the Walls Around Her Heart

I see so many of you wondering if you'll ever find the one, if love is truly going to happen to you.
The answer is yes – it comes to each of us.
The question I have for you is: "Are you open hearted and ready to embrace that love with your best self?"
True, love will find you when it's ready, not a moment sooner.
But, when your destiny does come calling, how will you embrace that chance?
Love may be blind, but you don't have to be.
The right person will never take advantage of you, mislead you and walk away – if they do, they were never "right" for you.
Ladies always seem so unsure what men want just as guys fail so often to grasp how to court a woman.
If you're holding out for "the one," don't be just another one night stand.
No gentleman will ever want what he can easily have – after all, the chase is part of the wonderful aspect of courting.
Leave him guessing, make him wonder, but don't play games.
A heart is meant to be loved, not played with – treat him as you'd want to be treated, but do so with some flair and pizazz all your own.
No one wants anything just handed to them – make him earn it.

If you want respect, loyalty and appreciation, give
what you expect and accept nothing less for
yourself.
Communicate your needs, but also listen to his.
Maybe it seems simple sometimes, like all he really
wants is food and sleep, but there's much more
there to be uncovered … if you're patient.
If you want him to dive deeper into your depths to
discover your truths, then reciprocate.
Help him verbalize the desires and dreams that
maybe he's never been able to communicate.
Be the lady that does more than try to love him.
Appreciate him and show it.
Respect him and tell him.
Learn who he truly is and express it.
Beneath the male bravado and macho tough exterior
may lie the sweetest heart you've ever known.
But if you're not willing to unravel his mysteries, then
you could just pass by the best man you've ever
met.
Maybe he cries at movies when you're not around.
Maybe he helps strangers when no one is looking.
Maybe he's been searching for you all his life, just
never knew how to look.
He makes the right choices and tries to love you …
in his way.
I've spoken often of what a gentleman should do,
but a true partnership only truly works if both people
do their part.
Don't expect him to understand your complexity,
help him learn the way to your soul, step by step.
Forever doesn't just magically appear for any of us,

it takes two people, falling in love,
Every single day.
Sometimes, it takes work, respect, compassion and sacrifice, but those who do what it takes will always find their way.
A man, a woman and a lifetime of possibilities.
It can find you when you least expect it in ways you never dreamed.
Don't just dream of love, be willing to work for it.
It won't be easy, it won't always be fun, but in the end, my friends,
It will always be worth it.
Your happily ever after will always start with you.

You Make My Heart Smile When Nothing Else Can

When I told you this was forever,
I knew what we would face.
Falling in love is easy;
Staying in love isn't.
We make mistakes, we rise and fall,
So long as we face them all together …
The hard days, the truly challenging ones,
Won't tear us apart.
In fact, it's those storms of life that will bring us closer together.
When the rains come crashing down on your heart,
know that I'm right there beside you,
Holding your hand and telling you everything will be okay.
We won't always have the answers and things won't ever be perfect,
But you'll always be perfect for me.
Protect, provide and profess:
I'll do all those for you and more.
Protect your heart as long as we both shall live.
Provide you with all the reasons to fall in love with me, all over again,
Every single day.
Profess my love for you through my words and actions …
Never will you doubt my loyalty and feelings for you.
So, let's make each other a promise:
To communicate through the problems,

To speak from the heart,
To smile through the pain,
To just be there for each other.
Home will always be your embrace.
In this life until there is no more,
That's all I could ever want and need.
Just you … forever.

If Only You Could Catch Her

She was a spirit that couldn't be tamed –
Though many had tried.
She sang the songs that filled her heart and danced
to the rhythm of her desires.
She might howl at the moon or lose herself in the
stars,
But she always immersed herself in the moments of
her life,
Free to love with the depths of her soul,
Celebrating her gypsy heart with beautiful abandon.
Rules didn't apply to her –
She made her own way and her own choices,
Listened to the whispers of her deepest secrets and
followed the whistling wind.
She would breathe in the sunlight and exhale in the
twilight.
She lived with reckless abandon and chased the
whims of her soul.
Her fire was intense and passionate.
You'd never forget her mischievous smile or her
boundless spirit,
Her impish giggle would reverberate in your mind
long after she floated out of your life.
She rose and fell as the tide ebbs and falls,
Choosing to heed the call of her dreams
as she chased the fading light of dusk.
Home was wherever she landed and the love she
doled out was powerful.
Once you looked her in the eyes and became
intoxicated with her soul, you'd never forget this wild

butterfly, weaver of dreams and gossamer magic.
But try as you might,
You'd never be able to catch this magical creature.
That's just how she loved … and lived.
Wild and free.
Catch her if you can.

Make Her Your Everything in Front of Everyone, Every Time

Ladies and gents,
Always strive to have the kind of love that isn't confined to the intimacy between two people.
Be proud of the connection you've built, the love you share and the relationship you've fostered.
We search so long and hard for the one to call our own that we sometimes think that the hard part is over once we've found them.
On the contrary, like all wonderful things, the best relationships are built on a foundation of trust, compassion, cooperation and passion.
Not once, twice or monthly, but every single day.
Don't be afraid to show your love off to the world – shout from the rooftops about how you truly feel.
It's not so much about what the world thinks anyways, but how amazing it makes your significant other feel to be appreciated in such a way.
The tango of life and love can be unpredictable and unbelievable, but we each have the capacity to love with unfettered devotion and unending loyalty.
Don't just dance with them in the kitchen, waltz with them through the daily challenges of life.
Make love with unbridled intimacy, engage your minds with unparalleled involvement, love your souls with unequaled depth.
To know love is to know each and every part of your partner – intellectual, emotional, physical and spiritual.
Don't neglect any part of each other in your

endeavor to forge a lasting foundation.
But whatever you do, however you choose to do it,
wherever you choose to do it ...
Always, always, always ...
Do it all with extreme passion.

To Truly Be in Love

Darlin',
When I told you I had fallen in love with you, those words failed to encompass the depths of my feelings for you.
There may not be any words in any language that can encapsulate what you mean to me and how you've changed my life … forever.
You whisked into my life from a world away, and I haven't been the same since – nor would I ever want to be.
Once you've been touched by the heart of an angel, how can you ever go back to the normalcy of a life without love?
One can't.
I won't.
Our love was unlike anything I'd ever known, though the meeting of our souls was so familiar – seemingly as if we'd loved in lives past and time beyond.
Sometimes … you just know.
It's incredible because you don't know how you know … only that you do.
A comfortable warmth that beckons you home – in those moments, you realize that you've found the mate of your soul in an unlikely way ...
But I'd have it no other way, would you?
The beckoning of an intimacy that defies reason, it's the catalyst for a passion that ignites every corner of your heart, mind and body ...
It permeates your thoughts and fuels your desires in a way that is strangely ... familiar.

No matter where we are or what the occasion, it takes only a subtle look from you, and in those moments, our eyes have an inviting conversation from across a room.

Swept away by your smile and intoxicated by the whisper from your heart, I cast aside judgement and reason as I reach your side.

Time slows and the world melts away as our lips collide and I pull you to me.

In that instant, as in all the time afterwards, you are all that matters.

You. Me. Us.

As I gaze into your eyes and wrap my arms around you, a conflicting peace envelopes my soul ...

While my senses are on fire ...

You, my love, are all I'll ever need.

Be the Man She Needs, and She Will Be the Woman You Want

Gentleman isn't a word,
it's more than a style,
it's more than a dress code.
It's an attitude,
it's a way of life,
it's a code of conduct.
Gentle on the outside yet savage on the inside.
Taking the high road while others choose to make
bad choices and live disrespectfully.
Personify the noble gentleman and embody the
patient wolf.
Know when to hold her hand and know when to pull
her hair.
She doesn't need flowers just on her good days,
she needs a warm embrace and a shoulder to cry on
after the bad ones.
Respect.
Honor.
Character.
Passion.
Those are the rare qualities that set a gentleman
apart from an average man.
It's not enough to know the way,
You must walk the path.
A man will tell her she's beautiful,
but a gentleman will make her believe it.
A gentleman will love passionately,
have a compassionate nature and

possess dispassionate judgement.
Gracious in manner and humble in tone,
a gentleman will always ...
open her door, hold her hand, and know the
difference between pride and insecure jealousy.
Touch her with your words,
pierce her with your eyes and
make love to her with your kiss.
Engage her mind, enflame her heart and
connect with her soul ...
A fancy watch won't make the time to act
respectfully,
but a gentleman will make the time for his lady.
The clothes do not grant one class,
for a gentleman wears anything with dignity.
Chivalry isn't dead, but it can't be bought, found or
borrowed.
It must be learned, practiced and applied.
Manners will open all the doors that even the best
pick-up lines won't.
She's a lady, not an object,
So treat her with courtesy, love her with passion and
listen to her respectfully.
Don't make her wait, chase or blush.
Unless, of course, it's behind closed doors.
There's a time for a gentleman ...
And then there's a time for the wolf.
She'll appreciate both ... greatly.
Neckties aren't just for adornment –
They are a bedroom accessory.
Help her understand why.

The Best Love

When I met you, I thought I had it all worked out.
I knew where I was going and had everything under control.
Truth is, I didn't even have a clue.
You turned right into left and upside down into right side ups.
You made me want to be a better man –
Not just for you, but for me as well.
For both of us, for our relationship, for our future.
You changed what I thought would make me happy and what made me smile.
We talk about nothing and laugh about the silliest things.
Conversations about deep feelings and laughter the bubbles up from sheer joy.
You showed me that being the best version of myself is what matters the most –
And what you truly loved about me.
You're my best friend who thinks my jokes are funny.
You're my soul mate who walks beside me in our life.
You're my lover who excites me with each kiss.
You're my daily reminder of how amazing life can truly be.
When I wake up and see your pretty face smiling at me, it just makes me realize ...
You made me believe again ...
In magic, in love and in you.
I wouldn't change a thing.
I love us for all the things we've been, we are and

always will be.
Most of all, because you'll always be mine.

Waiting for My Brave Dreamer

Honey,
All my life I've settled, compromised and made
excuses for the men in my life who didn't measure
up.
I sacrificed my dreams, put off my goals and went
the wrong way on a two way street.
I'm done with making someone else happy.
This time is mine to live, love and chase my dreams.
No more projects, only partners ...
I've never been a simple woman with ordinary
needs, but perhaps it's my fault for expecting those
men to be what I hoped they could become.
I need a man with far more than average hopes and
simple dreams.
I want a complex man who doesn't always live in the
moment.
It's hard to chase the wind when you don't know how
to see the unimaginable.
No, I learned the hard way that what I need is
exceedingly rare and exceptionally beautiful.
I deserve the fairy tale.
The dreamer who knows how to ground himself.
The gentleman who can unleash his wolf.
A man of action who can still live in the moment.
I want the things that are undefinable but necessary.
I want the passion to start a wildfire when we touch.
I need the chemistry to spark butterflies when we
kiss.
I am waiting for the man who doesn't see me with
his eyes, but, instead, his soul.

A compassionate lover who is moved by his soul and listens to his heart.
He won't just touch me, he'll feel me in all the ways the others never could.
So, I guess what I've realized is that I'm holding out for a hero,
A man that just, for lack of better words,
understands me and gets me.
Until he shows up, I got a lot of living and loving to do … starting with loving myself.
Who better to love me than me?

Those Quiet Times When the World Just Melts Away

It's those quiet times,
At the end of our day,
When the rest of the world slowly fades away.
Those are the moments I'll always cherish.
My arms around you, soaking in the events of the day,
Sharing my life with you.
It's not that it's always excitement and thunder,
It's that I get to spend it with you.
Your smile.
Your embrace.
Your love.
Talking intimately with the woman I love,
Grasping you in my arms ...
It sets my soul on fire.
I wish I had a magic power in those fleeting instants,
That I could make time stop as I gaze lovingly
Into your eyes,
So that I could love you longer,
Hold you tighter,
And squeeze those beautiful times like a warm blanket that grants such peace.
As we turn the pages of our story, these are the memories that I'll never forget.
The moments that I fell in love with you all over again, each and every time ...
... when I wished we could live forever
In those frozen moments of love.

I Want You Forever

They say there will be a moment when you know.
Across a crowded room, you glimpse at her, and all
you see midst the crowds of people … is her.
Your only thought in that instant is that you have
never seen anything so beautiful in your life.
Her smile and radiance drown out the world and all
you know as your mind races is that you can't
imagine spending your life anywhere else but in her
arms.
There's no rationale or reason that overcomes you
as your heart skips a beat and your breath stops –
only the absolute truth that she is the one.
Despite the turmoil that surrounds you and the
chaos of life that envelopes you at that split second:
that certainty – hers – calms your spirit and fills your
heart.
In that moment, you realize that every bad choice
and each failed relationship has led you exactly
where you needed to be.
You'd gladly kiss all the frogs again and try to make
all the glass slippers fit once more that were never
meant to … because you had to experience all the
wrong answers to understand the right one when it
finally found you.
The ifs and questions slowly fade away,
All that you know with complete certainty is that you
want to love her for the rest of your life.

Flawsome

Honey,
I don't expect everyone to get me, and I'm okay with that,
But feel free to give it your best shot.
I do things my way with my style, and frankly, it's unique.
That's the way I prefer it, owning my life the way I choose.
I don't follow the crowd and I don't like rules ...
But I'm awesome in all my own ways.
I embrace my flaws – in fact, I love my flaws and I wouldn't change anything about myself.
I take that back, there's one part of my puzzle I wish I could solve.
My heart.
I love too deeply and trust too much, and I've paid the price one too many times.
I put up walls, not to keep everyone else out, but to see who cares enough to tear them down.
I wish I didn't give everyone the benefit of the doubt, but I'd rather live with passion than be empty.
Here's the thing:
They'll tell you to be yourself, follow your heart and march to your own beat ... so long as they approve.
Forget that noise – I don't make ripples, I create waves.
They don't live my life and I don't owe anyone anything.
I don't need anyone's approval or acceptance.
Maybe I'm a beautiful disaster and complicated

mess and all that jazz..

But who cares?

I certainly don't.

At the end of the day, I love myself and who I am.

Rise or fall, I'm gonna keep shining bright like the shooting star I am.

My life?

It's perfectly flawsome.

I wouldn't change a thing about who I am, where I've been or where I'm going.

Anyone who thinks they can make me into what they want is knocking on the wrong door.

My heart, my soul and my spirit will remain carefree and strong until someone comes along that doesn't try to tame me ...

I'm worth the wait and much more.

The one who finally gets that won't need to know anything else –

I choose life, love and living with purpose.

Beautiful, wild and free.

I figure if I'm gonna do it, might as well do it my way.

So Much More than Those Three Little Words

They say that fairy tales aren't real and that dreams can't come true.
Things don't work out anymore for anyone and romance is dying … they'd have you know.
I never stopped chasing my dreams of love and wishing on stars that she'd show up ... and now I know why.
You can't make love show up before it's time and no amount of desire can alter what's meant to be.
It's hard, it's frustrating, but I know now that it's worth it – so very much so.
Looking into your eyes, I understand why all the others were all so wrong for me.
Hearing you say my name proved that all the naysayers never really "got it" about love, destiny and what's meant to be.
You can believe all your life that true love will find you, but until it does, it's just faith –
The hopes and dreams of fools, everyone would tell you.
Hoping that the one meant for you will show up is nothing more than a belief that you hold on to … deep down in your soul.
As time slowed and I felt your arms around me, I knew in that moment what "meant to be" truly felt like.
Come what may, from whatever broken road we may have traveled, all paths led us to each other.

That's not chance, hope or fortune.
All the heartache and broken promises just seemed to wash away as I pushed the hair away from your eyes.
In that moment, it all made sense.
You made everything … just make sense.
As if I'd known you, my love, all my life.
Almost as if I'd known the answer all along.
I turned to speak before you stopped me and smiled, saying simply …
"Of course."
In my heart, I knew you were perfect for me before I ever even asked.

Freeze Time

Darlin',
No matter where we are,
There are those moments in which I wish I could just
freeze time.
So I could steal away those beautiful emotions of
being in your arms and tuck them away ...
Little pockets of sunshine and happiness,
The joy of loving you in those instants is
immeasurable ...
I could live forever in the comforting embrace of your
love,
Wrapped up in a feeling of bliss that would be
endlessly enchanting.
There's nothing in this life so wonderful as the
feeling of your love in my arms, against my skin and
in my soul.
As our hearts beat in unison and souls collide,
My spirit soars with the knowledge that you'll always
be at the beginning and ending of all my days, for
there's nothing more precious and wonderful than
your outstretched arms waiting for me.
Waking up next to you and falling asleep in your
arms are two of the most amazing feelings I've ever
known ...
And I get to experience them each and every day
with the woman I love.
If I could capture that beauty of our love incarnate,
I would be a very rich man indeed ...
For having loved you would be the greatest treasure
of all.

Yet no money nor possessions could ever compare to the blessing I found in you.
The most valuable thing I will have ever have ... is and will always be your love.

The Heart that Beats Only for You

I don't always have to tell you that I love you –
I show you in the ways that I love you and what I do
– for you, with you, because of you –
the ways I cherish you without fail.
I never meant to fall in love with you, but
from the first smile to your last giggle,
you pretty much ruined that plan ...
and I couldn't be more okay with it if I tried.
When I seek meaning, you give me reason.
When I lose my way, you lead me back home, to
your arms.
When I wonder what tomorrow holds,
Your kiss shows me the future and all that can and
will be.
In truth, that's all I've ever wanted:
Love in my heart, hope for my spirit and belief in my
soul.
When I found you?
I found all that and so much more.
Thank you for all that you are ...
Most of all, thanks for the love that you give, the
person that you are and how you protect and
celebrate my heart ...
That will always light the way to our brightest of
tomorrows.
You give rhyme to the reason,
Sanity to the madness.
I could try to count all the ways I love you, but I'd
rather just show you –
Each and every day,

For the rest of our lives.
That's just one of the many reasons why my heart
will always and forever beat ...
Just for you.

Even the Most Beautiful Have Scratches and Scars

You were broken when I found you,
crumpled midst the emotional wreckage.
Life drained and heart broken, your soul wept
through each and every tear that fell.
But as I took your hand into mine, kissing your skin
with subtle purpose,
The storms in your eyes slowly began to subside.
You didn't want to believe in love, me or anyone.
Your spirit was crushed and your trust gone.
You needed a light midst the darkness that someone
had cast over your soul.
It's always darkest before dawn, I told you,
And the sun always rises.
Wiping away the tears, I smiled past your anguish
into the beauty that hid beyond.
Your reflection doesn't determine your self-worth,
and sometimes,
The most beautiful scars can create the most
wonderful heart.
They tell your journey, weave the amazing story that
is so uniquely you.
Scared and wounded, you wanted to trust me,
but you'd been burned that way before.
Your walls were high and your heart utterly bruised
from all the ones before.
Pushing aside your hair from your tear soaked
cheek, I softly kissed you, smiling warmly.
I can't make the pain go away and I can't make it all

better, but I can promise you to love you, unconditionally.

Sometimes, the hardest part of the journey is believing you're worth the trip.

You can't help what happens to you, but you can decide not to be reduced by it.

I kissed your forehead and stroked your hair lovingly as you weakly mustered a grin.

As our eyes met, souls truly alive for the first time together, I knew I'd forever live in those next moments as I spoke.

Even the brightest stars endure the darkest hours but when you're meant to become more, you find a way to light up the night sky.

"Baby, it's your time to shine."

And I knew in that moment you were finally ready ... you saw the path, felt the hope.

The look of recognition set in, and I saw the beautiful freedom in your eyes.

I saw more than a look, a moment or a truth.

I saw your soul.

In my eyes, in my arms, in my heart, at last ...

You had come home.

Gentlemen: Suit Up

Gentlemen:
There's a time for words, then there's a time for action.
You can tell her in endless ways that you love her, every day,
but there's a time when you have to stop telling and start showing her exactly what she means to you.
No phones, no television or movies.
Just your heart and hers … one on one.
Look into her eyes and feel the rhythm of her soul careen against yours in those moments.
Don't take her for granted and don't be lazy.
Do all the big things … take her to dinner, or even better, prepare a special meal for her.
Mix in the small gestures of love … notes on the mirror, flowers just because and texts that say simply ... "thinking of you."
Give her your complete focus and lose yourself in her arms.
Learn about her hopes, fears and dreams … and share yours.
Don't just be part of her life – share her life.
Uncover everything she is and you'll find an amazing person just wanting to love and be loved.
Take her hand in yours, hearts in unison and show her the path to forever, together.
It's then that maybe, just maybe, you'll understand that the true beauty of a woman –
is her heart, mind, body and soul.

Then remind her each and every day, in every way, how very much she is loved.

She Was Beautiful in a Way that Was Uniquely Her

When you find a beautiful wild spirit,
You don't try to catch or tame it.
Truth is, you probably couldn't, even if you wanted to.
Carefree and unique, a woman like her was the rarest of rare, and I very well knew it.
She'd cross your path and make your heart flutter … before vanishing moments later.
She'd love you and leave you breathless, stealing away your heart without the slightest warning.
I saw past her mystical smile and soulful eyes into a mystery that I knew I'd never understand but that wouldn't stop me from diving into all that she was.
Better to have love and lost, they say?
Gazing upon the gorgeous creature before me, I don't know that I could agree with that sentiment.
Strong, vibrant and willful, she redefined the entire concept of "unique."
I was lucky, some would say, to have caught the attention of such a wild thing for such a time, but I don't know that it was luck.
Meant to be comes to mind more than simple fortune.
How can I gaze upon the most amazing woman I've ever seen and let her go?
Truth be told, I can't.
I won't.
I'll walk beside her for as long as I might, make love

to her soul and drink in the moments I spend with her.

I'll tango with her spirit and protect her heart every day, in every way.

She's more than a woman, she's a wonderful adventure.

She's wild, she's free and she's a once in a lifetime woman.

I can't define her and I wouldn't dare try.

The most beautiful people are without definition or predictability … and that's just part of their charm.

All I can do is try to love her, and maybe, just maybe,

I'll dance with her heart, mind and soul until the last sands of our destiny whisks away unto nothingness.

It's a chance I'm willing to take.

She'll keep me wild … I'll keep her safe.

A happily ever after, her style, our way.

That's a fairy tale worth living.

And I Wonder, How Did I Find One So Perfect for Me?

When the still of the night settles around us,
And you're lying quietly on my chest,
I just soak in the beauty of the moment:
Your almost angelic breaths rising and falling,
As you drift off in peaceful slumber,
That's just one more reminder of all the ways I'm
thankful for you,
And simply can't believe that you're mine.
I watch you sleep and whisper all the things
that sometimes escape me when we're together.
I wish I was better with my feelings and words
sometimes, but I know you see how deeply I care for
you in my eyes, in my actions and how I love you ...
How very much you mean to me,
How you've changed my life and bettered my world.
How much you make me feel loved and special and
that every day
Is a joy and an adventure with you by my side.
Your soul found mine and together, we've never
looked back.
I try to reminisce to a time before you,
And honestly, all of those thoughts and feelings
escape me – almost as if they never even
happened.
Truthfully, nothing could ever compare to what we
found in each other and the love we share.
You're my true love, my everything and my safe
place.

As I brush away the wisps of hair from your peaceful face,
I can't help but radiate a warm smile from my heart.
You found me in a sea of people and made me complete,
Against all odds in a way that could only be fate and destiny.
I didn't really know what love felt like before you showed me, and now I can't imagine a life where I don't wake up beside you every day.
You were the answer to the question I didn't know how to ask,
The hope that I didn't know to dream for,
And the miracle that I couldn't have imagined.
I didn't even know how lost I was until you came knocking on my door,
Pulling on my heartstrings in a way that no one else could.
As I kiss your forehead and let my lips linger,
I realize for the millionth time,
Just how very blessed I am.
I'll love you until the horizon meets the sky and the ending of time.
I smile as I slip away into sleep,
Knowing I'll awaken to the best thing that's ever happened to me … you.

Kiss Her Mind but Penetrate Her Soul

At first glance, you might think she's an ordinary woman, but you couldn't be more wrong.

There's no such thing as an "ordinary woman" – only what you choose to see.

Beautifully complex and wonderfully chaotic, a woman can capture your heart, thrill your spirit and enchant your mind ... But that's just the beginning.

You think she's just a lady with simple needs –
Because you haven't really looked past her eyes ...
Into her soul.

You haven't plunged into the depths of her desires, hidden where few will see them ... until you dig deeper.

Reveal the secrets that she buries behind her walls ... And you'll begin to finally see her truth, you'll start to uncover the depths of her soul ...

The wonderfully undeniable but sometimes enigmatic scent of her inner beauty that will intoxicate you as you unravel her mystery.

The flesh yields so little of her essence,

That, until you delve deeper,

You won't begin to understand the wonder of the woman that she is underneath it all.

She has layers that unfold as the delicate rose ... peel them away to reveal the wonder of all that she is.

But make no mistake, she's the toughest version of delicate.

She doesn't settle for leftovers and expects your very best.

She won't compete for your attention and she'll never be "just an option."
She puts up walls not to keep others out,
But to see who cares enough to tear them down.
Her beauty truly just starts in the mirror ...
Each level you uncover reveals another layer of profundity that lies untouched and unloved.
Find her passions and you'll discover her heart.
Touch her heart and you'll see the gateway to her spirit.
Inspire her imagination, make love to her mind and penetrate her soul.
Do those things, venture where the other men before never cared to explore or made the effort –
Appreciate, respect and try to understand her.
And you'll find a beauty unlike any you've ever known.
That's when I suggest this:
Never let her forget she's loved.
Never let her forget she's beautiful.
Never let her forget she's special.
Most of all?
Never let her go.
You'll be glad you didn't.
Beyond the glitz and glamor,
Bad hair days and wondrous chaos,
She's a splendid mystery waiting to be unraveled.
You'll spend the rest of your life realizing why I say
... The real beauty of a woman is truly endless.

Never Let Him Go

Ladies,
If you're looking for a prince among frogs,
Start looking for the little things that will set him apart:
He opens the doors and pulls out your chair.
He treats others, even those he doesn't know, with respect.
He holds your hand and protects your heart.
Chivalry isn't a punchline to him, it's a guide.
Character isn't just a casual idea, it's a code of conduct that he values.
Events of your day, your dreams and fears ... he listens to them all.
He kisses you on the forehead and hugs you tightly.
Making you feel safe in his warm embrace is something you can't just create ...
It has to just happen ...
... and you all know what I mean.
Ladies, no offense, you're not always easy to understand ... but if he tries to, he cares.
Dancing in the kitchen or anywhere random isn't strange to him.
He says he's sorry: he values your relationship more than his ego.
Day trips to nowhere get him excited.
He's proud of you, your accomplishments and your relationship.
He holds your hand, protects your heart and makes love to your soul.
He tells you you're beautiful ... randomly.

He makes you laugh ... funny is better in pairs.

He wants to meet your family.

He send little notes and texts telling you that you're loved and that he can't wait to see you.

He's thoughtful.

He plans a date.

He runs his fingers through your hair as you're enjoying quiet time together.

If you just like doing nothing with him ...

He just might be a keeper.

The little things add up to being big things.

These are just a few of my favorite things.

There's indeed many more ideas to enjoy, display and contribute to the love affair between a man and a woman.

But every happily ever after starts with the heart of a lady and the love of a gentleman.

I'm Not a Maybe Kind of Girl

Sweetheart,
Let's get a few things straight.
I'm not into shallow lust or lukewarm love.
If you're not sure about me or don't know how you feel, then I'm not the gal for you.
I don't do anything halfway and I always play for keeps.
I don't know how to love with anything less than all of my heart and soul, each and every day.
I wear my heart on my sleeve, and my eyes will always speak a thousand thoughts that I can't quite find the words for.
I don't give my mind, body and soul to just anyone, but when I do, I'm all in.
Forever isn't just a fancy word in some vague fairy tale, it's what I'm holding out for.
It's what I want, what I deserve and I'm not settling for less.
It's more than an ideal, it's what love means to me.
If you're looking for one night, look elsewhere.
If you're hoping to capture all my nights, explore my days and uncover my truths, then hold my hand and let's talk.
I believe in promises.
I believe in deeds, not words.
I believe in doing what you say and saying what you mean.
If you're going to chase me, then be prepared to catch me if you're worthwhile.
I don't need anyone and I don't need love.

I have plenty of that for myself, and I'm happy doing my own thing.

Love isn't about what you need but what you want and deserve.

So, if you're not a "maybe" kind of guy and have the heart of a lion, the manners of a gentleman and the passion of a wildfire,

I'm all in.

Don't show me the stars.

Take me there.

Don't tell me about your dreams.

Let's chase them together.

Don't waste a moment of your time or mine if you're not sure.

If I'm what you want, know that love is forever and that tomorrow is promised to no one,

Then take my hand and let's go discover the wild places and make love under the bright moonlight.

Let's take trips to nowhere for all the reasons that matter and love fiercely, passionately and deeply.

This is my life and my dream.

All we need is a little love, a lot of belief and the world will be ours.

Tonight, we will be magical passion ...

Tomorrow, we can start building our forever.

The question is..

Are you all in?

Your Battle is My Battle, We Fight Together

I know you're the strongest person I've ever met,
but sometimes it's okay to not be tough.
You've spent your entire life fighting – to survive, to
make it, even just to be happy.
You're used to doing it all alone and never having
the partner and support you've always wanted but
never thought you needed … and definitely never
got.
I know you don't need me, because you're a survivor
… You can withstand any storm and outlast any
tough times, of that I have no doubt.
But the thing is, I'm here now.
You don't have to conquer the world all by yourself
because you're not alone anymore and you won't
ever be again.
I'm here by choice, and I'll always stand right beside
you, your hand in mine, so long as you'll have me.
So, what I'm trying to tell you is that you don't have
to be the strong one all the time.
It's okay to let your guard down and let me be strong
for both of us.
For you, for us, I can always be the toughest fighter
and warrior that pushes us through the challenges of
life and leads our way each and every day.
You've been hurt, don't know how to trust someone
enough to let your guard down and I know why.
I get that about you, and I'm willing to be patient as I
love and support you and face the battles you fight –

because they're my battles now, too.

I'm willing to grow together, with me by your side as we charge ahead.

You're not alone and haven't been from the moment my eyes met yours on that fateful afternoon.

So, come what may, know that I'm here with you, bracing for whatever storms life may throw at us.

Together, there's nothing we can't do,

No dream we can't catch, and there'll never be a day that we don't live to the fullest.

You were once a warrior, survivor and alone.

This is a new day and you're in a new place.

Here, with me, you're more than you ever thought you'd be and I'm happier than I knew possible.

You were a dreamer and lover all along but were so consumed with fighting that you forgot how to live outside of the moment.

You're not alone any longer.

We are all the things you've always fought to find –
Finally complete.

Undeniably strong.

Lovingly devoted.

And in my arms, hearts beating together, we will be forever one.

Twice as strong, the future is limitless as we face it side by side.

Let's go set this life on fire,

Starting with tonight ...

And the love we're about to make.

She Loves Hard Because She Knows How It Feels to Be Loved So Little

She's been through the heartaches and heartbreaks and knows that nothing beautiful is had without risk. She's got high walls, both to protect her heart and also to see who cares enough to try to take them down.
She doesn't want a casual love or to be one of many – she knows she deserves to be the only one.
This time around, she won't settle and she won't accept less than the best.
She knows her worth and realizes the wait will be worth it.
But that's the thing … she's not sitting around holding out for a hero –
She's working on herself, bettering herself … loving herself.
She understands that's the most important of all.
Her friends think she's crazy for putting herself out there, but she knows that's what it will take to find her soulmate.
She loves like a firestorm –
Intense passion that will set any soul on fire – most of all, her own.
She lives with conviction and loves without regret, for she realizes that she has just one shot at this life and holds nothing back.
So, maybe destiny won't come calling today, tomorrow, or next week, but when her name is called, she'll embrace it with all her light.

She'll love hard when there's love to be had, because she's felt the pain of being unloved and forsaken.
She won't settle for a lackluster love and knows passion is crucial to what she needs.
She'll never visit that place again of accepting a mediocre love – she vows with courage in her spirit and resolve in her soul.
She realized what she deserved and she's not settling for anyone or anything less than what she truly wants.
So, she'll keep living her best life, finding her joy every day,
And when the time is meant to be, she'll do what she does best:
Love hard with all her heart.
She's writing her story with the ink of her soul, and this time,
She's going to create her very best happily ever after –
One dream, one chance, one love for the rest of her days.
And no matter what, she'll always love hard when there's love to be had.

A Partner Not a Project

Ladies,
This one's for you.
Don't settle for less than you deserve.
Forget the excuses and tragic back stories.
You can't save him and there's no reason why you should feel like you have to.
True, we all have challenges and it's wonderful to stand beside someone you care about through their trials and tribulations.
But …
There's a difference between having to fix someone and a person that just needs some support.
A partner isn't like a house.
Stay away from the fixer uppers and steer clear of the projects.
If he can't support you and stand strong as your equal, then you should find someone who can.
Fighting for someone who won't fight for themselves will become a full time job, and you deserve the fairy tale.
You deserve romance and the good times.
Never settle and don't make excuses.
Listen to your heart … and your head.
You already know the answer.
You'll spend so long trying to save him that you'll forget why you're even there to begin with.
Fight for your dreams.
Chase your miracles.
Believe in your future.
Just do it with the right partner, not the wrong

project.

Don't spend your life chasing waterfalls in rainstorms that never end.

Stop trying to hold out for hero that turns out to be a zero,

And start embracing the gentleman who just wants to be in your life.

Equals, lovers, soulmates and best friends don't come with a "fixer upper" tag.

They come into your life ready to love you in all the ways you deserve.

That's real, that's true and that's the kind of forever you should be holding out for.

You deserve a partner, not a project.

Love Her Tenderly, Passionately, Savagely

How do you love a woman?
Completely, utterly and madly.
Tenderly and softly so that she falls in love with your heart ... every day.
Loving kisses and gentle patience will draw her closer and caress her spirit.
Connect with her on every level in every way to fully appreciate and begin to understand the diverse complexity of a woman.
Give her passion, intensely woven into the tapestry of your embrace and set her soul on fire –
Don't treat her like eye candy, love her like soul food.
She'll crave your touch and long for your mercurial connection.
But ...
Steal her away behind closed doors and stoke the flames of her desire ...
Love her savagely and let loose her true primality ...
She'll devour you with consumptive fire and plunge herself into your wild depths.
Lower your walls and open your heart in a raw, visceral and true way – that's what she wants and needs.
Complete and honest love is madness,
But it is the emotional catalyst for our descent into euphoric pleasure that is without equal.
Romance her.

Listen to her.
Stimulate her –
Mentally, emotionally and physically.
Most of all, claim her powerfully.
If you do those things ...
She'll never want for anything ...
But a place in your arms, your heart and your life
forever.

The Love of a Woman Who Knows Her Own Worth

Honey,
Let's set the record straight.
I'm not your part time, some of the time or most of the time kind of gal.
I'll never accept being just "an option."
I'm not just a one in a million woman, I'm a once in a lifetime lady.
If you haven't been paying attention and you don't recognize my quality,
That's your loss, not mine.
I'm not sticking around anywhere or anyone trying to prove that I'm worth it.
I know who I am and what I'm capable of –
Anyone that doesn't value me won't get a second chance.
I don't need sympathy, apologies or regrets.
I need a strong partner and an even stronger relationship.
Save the mediocre and lukewarm for your convenience store coffee and well vodka.
I give what I get, and when it comes to my heart, that's going to be only the best.
My soul is too deep and my love is too strong to give it away so easily.
Life's too short to waste my time and energy waiting on someone to make time or understand I'm a priority.
Step up or step aside, my passion is reserved for the

ones in my life who get me ... really get me.

I've got a long list of dreams, hopes and goals, so take my hand if you're willing to share and support me ... and I'll do the same for all of yours.

Together, we can conquer the world.

Yep, you guessed that I'm fiery, passionate and independent.

I'm not for the faint of heart or weak minded.

If you've got to figure out if I'm worth the effort, don't blink too long, because I'll be on my way to the next success.

Call me feisty.

Label me hard to tame.

Think I'm difficult.

I'm all those things and some others you forgot:

Beautifully broken.

Impossibly amazing.

Incorrigibly wonderful.

You'll never find another one like me.

Question is ...

Are you up for the challenge?

I didn't just start a new story, I tore out all the pages and started a fresh new book.

Will you be just another chapter ... or part of my happily ever after?

The best love stories don't truly ever end.

That's what I'm waiting for, and I won't ever settle.

I'm not holding out for a hero, I'm planning on never needing one.

Just me and you, equal and forever – with love, respect and passion.

Can you roll with that?

The Hearts Knows When the Search Is Over

All her life, she had searched the world over,
Longing for love and hoping to find her happily ever after.
She turned over every stone, kissed every frog,
Looked around each corner … to no avail.

Possibly slowly turned into never,
All the hopes she once had seemed
To vanish with bad choices and even worse men.
She fretted as she wondered if "he" truly existed.
She started to think fairy tales didn't come true.

It was on a beautiful Sunday afternoon,
Out of nowhere and in a way completely
Unexpected, unbelievable and unanticipated.
She came face to face with a man who seemed … familiar.

His gaze met hers, souls found one other,
And in an instant, she knew a calm never before known.
His voice soothed her spirit,
His touch felt like, well, home.

All the doubts and insecurities melted away,
As if they had never even existed.
Her "never" transformed into "always,"
Her "not now" changed into "forever."

She learned the hardest lesson of all:
Love comes in its own time and own way,
You can't predict it or even understand it.
All you can do is cherish it when it arrives.

For when Cupid's arrow finds your heart,
You'll recognize in an instant that they are the one ...
Your true love, your soulmate, your forever twin
flame.
She smiled – she had finally kissed her last frog.
In the middle of an ordinary life, she had found a
fairy tale.

A Real Gentleman Would Never Make You Run in Heels

Gentlemen,
There are truths of which we should all be aware.
Never keep a lady waiting.
Don't disrespect her and expect her to appreciate
that sort of treatment.
She's a lady – not an option, a possibility or a
choice.
She deserves and wants your full and undivided
attention:
Failure to do so will ultimately leave you trying to win
her back.
She's not a prize or a possession to be won.
She's a wonderfully graceful and beautifully vibrant
soul that can enchant your mind and tickle your
senses.
Look her in the eye, hold her hand in the dark
and kiss her softly on the lips.
Tell her she's beautiful when she least feels it,
Show her she is special when she most needs it.
Umbrellas in the rain and your coat in the cold,
Be the man she needs and she will be the lady you
want.
Surprises don't need a reason or occasion,
Because you love her is the only reason you will
ever need ...
And the only reason she wants.
Take her out on the town,
Cuddle her up on the couch ...

But whatever you do, gentlemen,
Ask to take her hand to dance,
Show her love's last song,
Because you will feel it in her touch, see it in her eyes and
Seal it with a kiss.
Don't make her chase you or compete for your attention.
A real lady won't run after you in heels,
but then, a real gentleman wouldn't let her.

Promise Me That This Is Forever

My love,
Promise me that this is forever.
Promise me that no matter what tomorrow brings,
It will find me in your arms.
Promise me that we will face everything together,
hand in hand.
Promise me that we will always have silly times and
mad laughter.
Promise me that you'll always be my refuge from a
world that sometimes hurts.
Promise me that we will always remember to put
each other first.
Promise me that we'll never go to bed without each
other and never let a fight linger.
Promise me that you'll love me for me and always be
true to yourself and me.
Promise me the love to last for all ages, until I find
you in the next life.
Promise me that I can always count on you, to be all
the things we need.
Promise me that you'll protect my heart, nurture my
soul and nourish my spirit.
Promise me that we will always remember, every
day, why we fell in love ... and do it all over again.
Promise me that when the hairs go gray and
wrinkles line my face, that you'll love me as you
always have.
Promise me that you'll never give up on us, no
matter what challenges arise.
Promise me that you'll always respect you, me and

us.
Most of all …
Just promise me that this love is the one –
The last promise I'll ever want ...
Is to be loved by you, forever.
That's the only promise I'll ever need from you,
Now and for always.

Love Me from the Inside Out

When he left, he broke her ...
Or so he thought.
Truth was, at the time, she thought the same thing.
Shattered into countless pieces, she tried to pick up the pieces while trying to move on.
She lost herself in him because he made it seem safe and so easy ...
Only it wasn't so safe and the easy just disappeared with a single phrase.
"It's over."
He thought he wanted something different, believed she wasn't good enough for him,
he thought he was the one who deserved better.
He didn't know what he wanted, and she paid the price for that.
He couldn't have been more wrong about who she was and the strength she had.
She had lost her sense of self and who she was meant to be ...
She stopped living her life and started living his, for him.
But that all changed on a stormy Saturday that she cried so many times about.
He did her a favor by setting her free, pushing her away because he never really understood the beauty of her soul – who loved him unconditionally.
He opened her eyes to who she was and what she wanted.
She wasn't an object, a toy or a hobby.
The love she had known wasn't really love at all – it

was bending to his needs in his way without getting the respect she needed.

Their love wasn't a love at all ... and it definitely wasn't a two-way street.

She decided that she'd rather be soul food than eye candy.

Her journey now wasn't about becoming anything, It was about unbecoming everything that wasn't really her – and never was.

She'd rather be loved for her scars and flaws than admired for fake perfection.

Beautiful chaos instead of blatantly boring, She knew that she was capable of finding and deserving of so much more ...

She wanted the truth, no matter how harsh, instead of the lies that had once soothed her.

She realized that true beauty isn't about a pretty face and a nice figure, It's the depth of your soul and love in your heart.

The most beautiful makeup for a woman isn't found in a store, It's the passion in her heart, depth of her character and the allure of her soul.

She didn't just survive the fire, She became more than a candle in the wind – She roared like a damned wildfire.

He wanted arm candy without a voice and beauty without soul.

Luckily for her, his mistake was her blessing.

He woke her up to the gorgeous possibilities that lay before and within herself.

Beauty without depth is just window decor.

With all her mysterious scratches and disastrous
dents, she desired to be loved for who she truly was.
She realized finally,
That she wanted to be loved –
From the inside out.

Dream of Me While I'm Away

There was something so different about him,
something she couldn't quite put her finger on.
The way he moved,
The way he talked,
The way he respected and listened to her,
The way he made her feel like she was the most
beautiful and special woman in the world.
No matter the day,
Regardless of how and why,
He could reach across any distance and touch her
heart with only a few simple words.
"Good morning beautiful" meant something so very
different than it ever had before.
"Good night, love" was always the perfect way to
end any night and something she wanted when she
couldn't have him instead.
He didn't have to be beside her to be there with her
– she had his love tucked away in her heart, always.
He didn't kiss her lips, but her soul.
He didn't touch her skin, but melted her heart.
He didn't just love her, he made her feel adored.
He looked at her the way she had always dreamt of,
and that's how she knew he was ...
The one she had waited a lifetime for.
He was the answer to the question she had been
afraid to ask –
Was this meant to be?
Could he really be the one?
She was almost too afraid to ask lest she ruin the
perfection of their love.

All it took was his smile, a promise and how he loved her, each and every day ...
Her heart knew even before she did.
He was the man she wanted for always.
He didn't just love her.
He didn't just make her feel special,
He did something no one else had ever done.
He treated her in a way she had never known – with love, respect, passion and understanding.
He completed her, cherished and helped her understand ...
Love is a gift ... a promise she would never forget.
It was a blessing she planned to spend the rest of their lives enjoying by his side ...
Just the way she'd always wanted.

I Want the Breather of My Soul … My Light Bringer … My Soulmate

Honey,

If I had a dollar for every time I've been asked why I'm single, I would be filthy rich.

Most of them look at me and just don't understand.

They think something must be wrong with me …

That I'm hard to please, don't have it together or don't know what I want.

In fact, it's just the opposite.

It's really about what's right with me –

I'm not looking for one night or a short-term solution.

While everyone else around me was settling, making do and finding excuses for their project partner, I was evolving.

When so many suitors chased me for a single night, I held firm to my ideals and what I wanted.

I didn't want just a lover.

I don't need just anyone.

I want and need the one – my person.

My soulmate.

My twin flame.

My best friend.

My partner in crime.

My forever love.

Sure, I could have made the choice a long time ago and taken the best of who came along, but that's not how I'm wired.

I love with all my heart, and I don't settle for anyone who can't light my soul on fire.

I'm not passive, soft or insecure, I'm a dreamer with passion.

Don't get me wrong, I'm not saying I don't want to settle down, and I'd love to find my missing piece ...

But I won't accept just anyone.

If they're not the one, then I'm not interested.

If they don't know what they want, then I'm walking the other way.

Dating for fun and loving aimlessly is for everyone else.

I want the kind of love that curls your toes when you kiss them.

I crave the butterflies when you hear their voice.

I search for that one man that can melt me with his eyes, his touch and his kiss.

I need the sort of magic that makes you believe that together, you can do anything.

I don't have all the answers and sometimes, I'm a complete mess, but I'm always sure of who I am and what I want.

I'm not going to accept just any old version of a fairy tale, I'm writing my own take on happily ever after.

I don't need saving nor do I need to be fixed.

I'm beautiful just the way I am.

If someone can't appreciate me for me, then I don't need them in my life.

Maybe, just maybe, in this story, the damsel and hero walk side by side into the sunset.

Dreams do come true and magic is real.

I've seen both, and if you're the one for me, take my hand and let's go adventure to impossible places and ride the wind.

Let's go make the kind of love that they write songs about.
The night is young and our spirits are indomitable.
Let's go find our forever ... one dream at a time.
Are you game for a life and love that'll make you never look back?
I'm down for that, if you can keep up.
Catch me if you can ... I'm worth it.

A Gentleman Knows

Guys, the message is very clear.
Be a gentleman, even when no one is there.
Having honor is a choice.
Treat her with respect – every day.
Open her door,
carry her umbrella.
Hold out your hand as she ascends the stairs,
Take her coat.
Pull out her chair.
It's not about the love poems and diamond rings,
But about the gestures that come from the heart.
You'll learn that the little things are the big things after all.
Doing more than just saying the right things, but following through.
Sometimes, she doesn't need you to solve her problems, she needs you to pull her close and just listen.
Hold her hand, protect her heart and nourish her soul.
Choose to be more while the others decide to be less.
Don't be a man of words, vow to be a gentleman of action.
Anyone can promise the sun, moon and stars ...
But a gentleman will be the one that ropes the stars and brings them home to her.
Words and action with integrity.
Be the one who rises above and makes her feel like she's everything, and she'll do the same for you.

When all else fails,
Don't get her a gift card.
Buy her some shoes.
Heels.
Open toe with straps.
Probably black or red.
She'll love you almost as much as she loves the shoes.

But What if You Fly?

Darlin,
I know you're afraid.
Afraid to feel, to trust, to believe in love again.
I realize it's been so long since you've felt safe.
I know feelings are scary, and the thought of letting
someone in can be terrifying.
Your heart has been bruised and broken, and you
don't know if you'll ever be able to love completely
again.
You lost yourself for a while and don't exactly know
the road back.
There's no easy answer nor safe path when it
comes to love, and I get that.
I can't promise you that pleasure comes without
some pain,
Because sometimes, even the deepest love comes
with the hardest lessons.
It's a risk that I can promise you comes with the
most beautiful rewards.
It's so hard to take that first step,
to release your heart and start taking down your
walls.
When you're standing at the edge of the abyss,
sometimes all you can see is the darkness you're
afraid to lose yourself in again.
You've had your heart broken and your soul
shattered before,
So I understand every fear that screams out from
behind your eyes.
Take my hand in yours and start to believe, close

your eyes and take a deep breath.

Let's take this one day at a time, small steps to learning, growing and trusting each other.

It's darkest before dawn and storms precede every rainbow,

But it won't rain forever.

You've come so far and endured so much to become the beautiful person you are today ...

Now it's time to slowly begin, day by day, opening your heart up to the possibility of more.

More chances.

More life.

More happiness.

More love.

Breathe in the possibilities and expand your mind as the wind of hope starts to blow.

The smallest of smiles creeps into the corners of your mouth as you close your eyes and start to believe that maybe, just maybe, I might be for real – that true and lasting love might actually be possible.

"But what if I fall?" you ask.

Oh, my Darlin', but what if you fly?

You Are My Happy Place

My love ~
At the end of the day,
When the world has behaved badly,
Forced tears to your eyes,
Know that I'll always be waiting.
To hold you tightly,
Wipe away your sorrows,
And just listen.
Rainy days will come and go,
The winds of change will try to tear us apart,
But together, we can overcome it all.
What the world doesn't know,

Is that it's already written in the wind,
In the sun's baleful glare,
In the snowfall's soft whisper,
In the resurgence of Love's sweet song,
In the sure fading of Life's gentle breath,

That you and I were meant to be.
Nothing in this life or the next can rip asunder
What time and fate already know ...
That's our simple truth.
I've loved you across countless lifetimes
And always found you against any odds.
My one truth and living legacy,
I'll forever be right there,
Loving you.

p.s. Thank you to my mother, who penned the middle stanza in a letter to me, which fit so wonderfully in this piece.
Love you, Mom.

Be With a Man Who Messes Up Your Lipstick, Not Your Mascara

Honey,
Let's get some things straight.
I'm not your average woman and I won't accept just any sort of treatment.
I don't settle for less than the best, and I'll expect that from you.
Don't treat me like an option and expect me to make you a priority.
I give what I get, and I do it 24/7.
I may think and carry myself like a lady, but I'm not like any woman you've ever known.
I make my own money and get my own back and don't ask anything but loyalty in return.
I expect nothing but your utmost respect, decency and gentlemanly behavior.
Don't call me sexy, hot or babe if we're not involved ... those are the words reserved for one man: my true love and partner.
Don't be crass, crude or disrespectful unless you want to find yourself on the other end of a one way conversation.
You might think I'm high maintenance or have fancy taste, and that's true ... because I maintain myself and pay my own way.
I'm not difficult, challenging or stubborn.
I'm sassy, feisty and fiery.
I'm not asking you to understand me all the time ... I don't even know how to do that.

I am asking you to be a gentleman, be classy and courteous and do all the things the others won't.
I'm too much for most men, and weak men can't handle me, so do us both a favor and step it up.
Be one of the good guys:
Open my door, take my coat, pull out my chair.
Put the man in manners, sweetheart.
Take initiative and plan things for us – what lady doesn't love a surprise?
I plan on living and loving my way, not the way the world thinks I should.
Others might mistakenly call me loud, opinionated or bossy.
They just don't know what to make of me.
I think like a lady but roll like a boss.
I don't have time for excuses, settling or accepting second best.
I let them think what they want and do what I want anyways.
I'll always be classy, sassy and a little badassy.
It's part of my charm and my charisma.
I'm wanted by many, taken by none because I'm waiting for the one.
I'm a fiery gal with a deep soul and a lioness spirit, but there's no lie in my fire.
I'm spunky, sassy and strong willed, but I'll always be loyal, real and truthful.
I give what I get … and more.
Assuming I was like most women was your first mistake.
Treating me like most women will be your second.
I don't stick around for the third.

If you can't mess up my lipstick before you ruin my mascara, then it's pretty simple ...
Game over, baby.
There aren't second chances when you break my heart before you even melt it.
I deserve the best.
That's all I'll accept ... end of story.
Can you handle that?

She Was Strong, But Her Heart Was Weary

She was the one that everyone thought was always happy.
She was so strong, and people admired her for that.
The thing is, there were tears behind her eyes,
Fears behind her heart and pain behind her laughter.
She covered up the scars of a hard life,
and she built a wall around her oft broken heart.
So many nights, she cried herself to sleep,
Nursed a glass of wine through the sadness,
Picked up the pieces alone because she had to – for herself, for her loved ones.
She made her own joy and fought for her laughter.
Love frightened her because, frankly, it always left her heart crushed into countless pieces.
She was beautifully damaged in all the ways that she chose and celebrated.
Her soul bore the scars of her passionate life,
And she'd tell you that she'd never change a thing if she had to do it all over again.
That's just who she was – no apologies, no regrets.
She loved fiercely, lived courageously and found her way through the pain.
Even when her demons screamed loudest,
They couldn't steal her joy – she wouldn't let them.
She was powerful not because she wasn't scared or worried – she often was –
But because she always found a way to rise above,

despite her fears.

She didn't seek love, because that scared her most of all …

She didn't think she could bear one more heartbreak or disappointment.

Her fragile heart was bruised and battered,

But she refused to give up on love.

She hoped when most wouldn't.

She dreamed when others couldn't.

Most of all,

She loved when anyone else wouldn't have.

So, until she found her purpose, and until real love finally came calling,

She'd smile through the pain,

Laugh through the tears,

Fight through the fears.

She became the fire that once had tried to consume her,

Waiting for the one who was willing to risk being burned,

The man who would love her in spite of her jagged edges and often fiery disposition.

Sooner or later, she'd find someone who'd finally understand her in the way she wanted:

She didn't need to be tamed.

She just needed to be loved on her terms.

Love is Seeing an Imperfect Perfectly

Love isn't perfect,
it's not always on your schedule and it can be
unpredictable.
You can't pick the one who captures your heart or
how they do so.
Sometimes, love shows up when you least expect it.
Embrace it, don't try to understand it and give it a
chance.
Follow your heart but don't forget your head.
Truth is, you don't pick love, it picks you.
Your soulmate may come into your life in their own
style, unexpectedly.
But that's just the beautiful part of destiny,
It comes calling when the time is right for your heart.
You'll never be perfect and neither will your true
love.
No one is perfect, now or ever.
But that's the wonder of love ...
because they just might be perfect for you.
True love is absolute acceptance of someone for
who they truly are –
Flaws, scars and ugly truths:
We welcome all the shattered pieces and emotional
scars when we truly love someone.
We want to hug them tightly ...
Because in our arms, everything broken becomes
whole again.
Two hearts join as one when it's meant to be.
Love isn't blind but it's true, it's honest and it's
always faithful.

The loyal heart will always look past your imperfections and see your soul.
That's where true love lives –
Perfectly imperfect in all its glory.
Embrace your flaws and all your baggage on your journey to chasing dreams together.
Life is always better when shared with someone you love.
Choose a full life.
Choose passionate love.
You'll be glad each and every day that you did.
It'll be risky, it won't be easy, but it will always be worth it in the end.
What's meant to be will always find a way … if you decide to let it be.

I'm Not Responsible for Who You Imagine Me to Be

Sweetheart,

Let me tell you exactly who I am and where I stand.
I know what I want, what I deserve and I won't settle for anything or anyone less than that.
You see, the ones before, they tried to change me into what they wanted.
They refused to see who I was and appreciate me for everything I'd worked hard to become ...
And that's their loss.
Yes, I'm flawed, imperfect and a complete mess sometimes, but I'm always me.
I don't play games, and you can count on me to always be real and authentic.
I give what I get and I'll always give my partner all of my heart and loyalty.
I will never fight for your attention or chase you to be with me –
I know my self-worth, and I'm worthy of someone willing to put me first and be there for me.
Love isn't a part-time choice, and my heart isn't an option – it's a priority.
I know what makes a relationship successful, and I'm willing to put in the work.
If you're a player trying to run a game with me, then let me be the first to change the rules and walk away ... My heart and love will never be "up for grabs."
If you can appreciate, support and respect a strong woman, then let's see what adventures we can lose

ourselves in.

If you're insecure, jealous or superficial, then hit the door to join the rest of the immature boys.

I want to live with passion, love with devotion and write my happily ever after with someone who really gets me.

So, if you're thinking that you're going to make me into something you want or try to change me, then here's your wake-up call.

I evolve to become a better person if I choose, not to try to please anyone.

Even the brightest diamonds were forged under pressure, so it's my time to shine.

If you want to share the spotlight, chase our dreams and radiate brightly together, I'm all in.

The question is, can you handle my truth?

Be the Reason that She Believes Chivalry is Still Alive

Ladies and gents,
Here are some truths that I consider essential:
Build the proper foundations for love and your relationship,
Make her a priority, never just an option.
Never be lazy in love, endeavor every day to make her fall for you, all over again.
Use all the big ways – and little ways too – to remind her why you have her heart.
Don't give her a reason to doubt your love for her, instead give her all the reasons to believe in your heart, soul and devotion.
Listen to her, her heart and her dreams.
Encourage her, support her, but more than anything, just be there for her.
She's not always looking for you to solve her problems, sometimes she just wants you to listen … not a man's forte.
You may never understand her, but it doesn't mean you should stop trying to unravel her mystery.
Support her present, encourage her future and understand her past.
Love isn't judgmental, and you shouldn't be either.
We all have our flaws and history …
accept her and appreciate the woman she's worked hard to become.
Chances are, she's scratched and clawed to evolve and achieve who she is – always remember and

celebrate that.

Be romantic – not just in the big ways but all the little ones as well.

It's not always about flowers, lavish gifts and amazing trips ... those are wonderful gestures ...

But it's the little things that make her heart smile:

A note telling her that you love her.

A text or call just to let her know you were thinking of her.

Cook dinner for her.

Dance with her in the kitchen.

Bring her breakfast in bed.

Hold the door for her.

Just tell her that she's beautiful, often – inside and out.

Anyone can compliment her beauty ... be the man who appreciates her heart, spirit and soul.

You'd be surprised how just reaching over and holding her hand will make her smile.

A guy will speak.

A man will explain.

A gentleman will inspire.

Be the reason that she forgets her heart was ever broken,

The man that helps her to believe in love again.

Be patient with her as she slowly takes down the walls around her heart –

Use those blocks to build a strong foundation for your relationship.

If you're the man she needs, then she will be the lady you want.

Don't substitute crass for class,

And don't accept just any woman –
Hold out for the lady of your dreams.
Not a one in a million girl,
But a once in a lifetime lady.
Take your chance to step up
And be the one man ...
Who shows her that true love is real ...
And that fairy tales do come true.

Love Like There is No Midnight & Fairy Tales Do Come True

*For all those holding out for their happily ever after,
don't stop believing – it will happen
when you least expect it.*

I don't care what "they" say.
I want a fairy tale.
I deserve happily ever after and once upon a time.
I need the love affair that will take my breath away.
They don't dare to dream.
I do.
I will have the love story that redefines the fairy tale.
Kisses in the rain and embraces in the dark.
Yes.
Chivalry is still alive and dreams do come true.
I want out of the labels into a class of my own – I
don't believe in fitting into boxes, those are for the
unimaginative.
"They" haven't kissed an angel – they don't know
what forever looks and feels like.
I have.
Passionate kisses, warm hugs and the look in her
eyes that melts my heart.
So, don't tell me I can't have an old fashioned
romance that never ends ...
Because I can. I will.
I do.
The kind of love that people see and smile, because

they know.

They don't have to ask how or if, they just get it – they can see it in our eyes.

She'll be the type of lady who lights up a room when she walks in and brightens my smile.

When I look at her from across the way, I know one thing: she's the one.

I won't settle for anything less, and I don't have to.

True love and forever are real if you just know how to believe and have faith … and an open heart.

I believe in true love, in soulmates, in twin flames.

I believe that we find the one when we are meant to, chance doesn't tell us the ending to our story.

We do – if we are open-hearted and able to believe.

So, when I tell you I want the fairy tale, and the last first kiss ever, believe it.

I'm not asking anyone but one to share my dream, because "they" will never understand the true power of a love story like ours ...

And it's okay, no one else has to.

So long as I have you in my arms and our love in my heart, I know that we can do anything, together.

Until you catch a taste of heaven on the lips of an angel, you don't how amazing that kind of love truly is.

It doesn't just change the moment or the kiss, it transforms everything: your heart, your dreams and your life.

Once upon a time and happily ever after, our fairy tale love story started with a look and ended with forever.

You made all my dreams come true in a single kiss.

The next chapter ... in the rest of our lives.
Then, I'll find you sooner in the next life once more
... So I can love you longer –
True love stories never end.

Asking Him to Love Her

She had waited her whole life,
Always hoping, never knowing, always believing.
She was a complex girl with a simple wish.
True love, for a lifetime, evermore.

She endured more times of heartache and
heartbreak
Than she ever cared to reminisce about.
She never stopped believing that at the end
Of her struggles was the love she dreamt of.

She read the stories and cried through the movies,
As others all around her fell in love,
So effortlessly it seemed at times.
She tried not to despair and lose hope,
Because she always knew her time would come.

She knew that it was easy to stop hoping
When the path to love always dead ended in
heartbreak.
She overcame the disappointment, the hurt and the
sadness
Of men she thought could be "the one"
With the beautiful light she had in her soul.

It was never a matter of how, when or who,
Because she knew her story was written long ago in
the stars,
Love was more than her hope and dream,
It was her lifelong destiny.

She didn't need any man, but she did want her
soulmate.

So, when she saw a man unlike any other,
Her heart leapt and her soul smiled,
For somehow, in some way, she just knew.
That this was somehow different and special –
He was the one meant for her for always.

When the moment came, heart to heart,
It became very clear as his soul whispered to her,
That what's meant to be will always find a way.

After all the broken roads and painful tears,
Her heart sighed and she smiled because she knew:
She was just a girl, standing in front of a boy,
Asking him to love her.

And Then ... She Rose Again

I'm not a failure but I've failed.
I'm not a mistake but I've screwed up.
I'm not a disaster but I don't always get it right.
Truth be told,
I've fallen more times than I can count, and I'm okay
with that – I learned from each failure.
I've stumbled, failed and made more mistakes than
most people,
But then, I'm not like most people ...
They haven't had to claw and scratch to find their
way, to survive, just to be happy.
I had to be strong when I thought I had nothing left
because I didn't have any other options.
I surrendered everything that I was to become who I
was meant to be.
The critics don't know what it means to be at the end
of their rope and not know where to turn.
But you see, that's where my story begins – where
everyone else's tale stops.
I didn't just crash and burn,
I fell and crashed into a million pieces.
I shattered in ways that most can never recover
from, but that's the beauty of my story –
It's a tale of massive failures and anguishing
struggle,
It's a journey of broken hearts and wounded wings
... But more than that,
My path is a story of triumph amongst the tragedy,
Rising from the ashes and finding myself when, not
long before, I couldn't even find my way.

It's a rekindling of my fire when my spark was almost gone.
There were many times I was down and out,
So lost in the darkness I couldn't even see the light
... But that's what makes me who I am and part of my indomitable spirit.
I uncovered my strength and unleashed my courage.
I clawed my way out of the abyss into the light.
I didn't know how I'd make it some days, but somehow I always found a way.
I don't need help up, and I don't want a handout.
You can keep your sympathy, I'm gorgeous in all the ways that matter ... deep and soulful.
I want someone to walk beside me and appreciate everything that went into making me, the beautifully broken heart that roared back from the fire.
Equal, no more and no less.
Love me for me and all my splendid chaos, and you'll begin to understand the fire in my heart.
I have magic in my spirit and a passion in my heart that nothing can take away from me.
So, honey, understand that life may knock me down, and I'll have to fight harder some days,
But you can't keep a strong person down, ever.
So, stand with me or stand aside, I have places to go and dreams to catch.
Like most wild creatures,
I was always meant to be free.
These wings ... they're made to soar.
Love me the way that I deserve or let me go ... you'll never keep me in a cage when I'm meant to fly high.

Not Just a Lady, a Legend

Don't be just a woman, be a lady ...
More than that, be a legend.
And if you can do it rocking heels and a great outfit,
do that too.
After all, a gal can't conquer the world without her
own style and the shoes to match, right?
Don't ever forget to keep your head, heels and
standards high.
If they can't keep up with you,
If they don't understand that you're one of a kind
amazing, then you're better off without them.
Don't ever let anyone dull your sparkle.
The brightest diamonds are forged under the
hardest pressure ... and it's your time to shine.
You made it through the rest, so don't settle for less
than the very best.
You deserve it.

Forgetting Yesterday & Dreaming of Tomorrow

Once upon a time,
I didn't believe in fairy tales, true love or happily ever after.
I had been hurt more times than I could count,
Found all the dead ends in search of love.
It seemed that each time I got my hopes up,
They were dashed just as quickly.
I'd look around and see the couples in love,
dismayed at the proclamations of feelings everyone else shared ...
That I seemed destined to never know for myself.
That's a lonely place, you know?
One piece of a jigsaw meant for two, even if you don't quite truly believe that you'll ever find "the one"
... it's hard to be solo when you're missing something you can't quite put your finger on.
So, you sing all the love songs, read all the love stories and wistfully make wishes on every shooting star.
You can be in a room full of people and feel utterly and completely alone.
Not that the others don't love you, make you feel unaccepted or leave you out ...
But it's just not the same as sharing it with that special someone.
You see, though, I never stopped believing that she was out there ...
And one afternoon, everything changed.

Left became right and up turned into down.
Truthfully?
I've never been so happy to be completely breathless as I was in those moments.
The moment I saw my future waiting for me as I walked through the door.
The moment I fell in love as I saw you for the very first time.
The moment I recognized what forever tasted like when I kissed your lips.
You see, it's in those life changing instants when you happen upon the one meant to share your life that all the failures of love lost and broken roads melt away.
The lonely nights and disappointment all just make sense as I take you into my arms and finally find refuge in the embrace that I've waited my entire life for: yours.
We'll look back many years from now and know that was the beginning of forever.
I told you that I would marry you on the very first night we met, and though you thought me crazy ...
Perhaps I thought so a little as well –
It turns out maybe I wasn't so crazy after all, because I recognized my future in you.
When you know ... you just know.
And as I fall asleep every night with your face resting on my chest, I couldn't be more thankful for the broken roads ...
That led me straight to you.

Distance Doesn't Separate People – Silence Does

As the rain cascades down,
I reflect upon my life, my past ... you.
I wonder what you're thinking,
What you're doing right now.
Are you laughing about something silly,
Or are you enjoying life?
I can't help but think about why you're not here, in my arms.
I don't know where we lost our way,
But something happened and we stopped.
Somehow time and life just pushed us apart.
I wish I knew the answers to all the reasons
Why we don't talk anymore,
I just know that we don't.
I miss you.
I miss your voice, your laughter and your goodnights.
I miss the way you say my name and make me smile.
I miss the way your lips curl when you're happy.
I miss the smell of you on my clothes and the feeling of you pressed tightly against me.
I miss your hugs and the how you brightened my days.
Life just isn't the same without you in it,
And I can't turn back time to bring you here.
As I sit and reflect upon our love that was, our life that could have been and the hope that I still have,

I try to think back to the good times, to envision our laughter and love, the things that always make me smile.

I hold onto those memories and squeeze them tightly,

For that's what gets me through days like this.

When all it seems to do is rain, I fight back the emotions and imagine you're with me again.

I close my eyes, and you're there, pulling me in, kissing my lips and loving me again.

So, until I drift off into slumber once more,

I'll smile and think of those beautiful dreams,

Where you still love me like you once did.

For me, until love finds me once more, that will have to be enough.

Maybe it will be you that the west wind blows back into my life, maybe not.

What's meant to be will always find a way, and maybe we won't ever be "us" again, and I'm okay with that.

Regardless, I still have our memories, the dreams we shared and the hope for the future that I'll never abandon.

For a time, it was love, it was us, and it was beautiful.

The Heart of a Warrior Maiden

Honey,
I realized a long time ago that being just beautiful or pretty would never be enough.
There will always be someone newer, younger and prettier around every corner.
I'm brave enough to be real in a world that already has too many fake people.
I'll always be real, authentic and genuine even though that's too much for some people.
I'm going to redefine "beautiful" with my own style, taste and attitude.
True beauty isn't about looks, clothes or curves, it's so much more than that:
It's about depth of soul, quality of character and fierceness of heart.
I'll never be "just a woman." I'm so much more than that.
One word will never define me, and I wouldn't have it any other way.
I'm strong enough to shine brightly and confident enough to own it.
I'm bold enough to be heard and smart enough to make my voice matter.
Forget the fake eyelashes, fake tan and all the rest of the countless other kinds of fake.
I'm going to be real, gritty and honest.
I love who I am regardless of who else does –
I don't need anyone's approval.
I'll always be far from perfect, but that's the best thing about me …

I'm flawsome –
Flawfully awesome in all the ways that are meaningful.
I'm constantly a work in progress, and that's the key word: work.
I work at evolving.
I work at being my best.
I work at surviving the hard days.
I work at being a great friend, person and partner.
I don't ask for charity and I don't live with regret.
Sure, I put up walls around my heart, but not for the reasons everyone always thinks.
I don't care about keeping anyone out, rather I want to see who cares enough to tear them down.
I'm tough, I'm independent and I've been broken more times than I can count.
But you see, sweetheart, that's the thing about a survivor.
I don't quit.
I don't know how to fail.
I don't take anything from anyone, and I never settle for less than I deserve.
People in my life are there because I choose for them to stay.
I learned a long time ago, everyone comes into your life for a reason, a season or a lifetime.
Some may come and go, others will teach you a lesson before they go,
But the rest will be there for life – I'll hold them close to my heart.
I'll always be sassy, classy and spunky, but I'm unapologetically real.

So, when you meet me, you may think I'm many things, maybe even beautiful ...
But it won't be for my makeup, hair and nails.
It will be for the sparkle in my eye, the glow in my heart and the fire in my soul.
That's the kind of beauty that's unforgettable, and that's exactly who and what I am.
Catch me if you can ...

I Don't Want the Heavens or the Shooting Stars … I Want to Love and Be Loved

Darlin',
When I say that I love you,
I'm trying to say so much more than those three little words convey.
I'm trying to tell you how very special you are to me, how you mean more than anything else.
I'm trying to express how deeply I care for you, and how much I love the times we share.
I'm trying to share how much I trust you, need you and know that I'll always be there for you.
I'm trying to relate how much I depend on you and wouldn't want to face life without you.
There aren't words that can truly define the way I feel about you, but I hope you can tell –
In the way I look at you with complete adoration,
In the way I will always put your needs first,
And how very much I look forward to coming home to your arms.
In the way I think of you when you're not beside me, with a love note, a text or a passing thought …
You can't cross my mind because you never leave it.
So, each time that I take your face in my hands and smile,
Saying those three words that encompass so much more,
Know that "I love you" is my daily proclamation of how grateful I am for you, how much I appreciate all

that you do for us,
And how I can't wait to spend the rest of my life
loving you.
You are and always will be my forever person.
I love you.

Quiet Her Thoughts and Ease Her Soul

When the night falls and her thoughts rage,
She yearns for the calm midst her inner storm.
As her emotions run rampant,
A tumultuous roller coaster of feelings
Sometimes wreaks havoc on her heart.

She feels the worst and hopes for the best,
But the trust that has been broken before
Crashes and breaks against the walls of her heart,
Always wanting, never knowing and ever hoping ...
For the one who can finally feel her soul.

Tentative and unsure, she cautiously begins –
To believe when her fears warn her away,
To hope when her mind tells her not to,
To love when her heart whispers "be careful."

Many have come and gone, all have failed.
She stands before him, soul bared and heart
healing, wondering if he could be the one,
To have and to hold until time is no more.
Her soul seeks him quietly in the dark.

She doesn't want to believe,
She can't risk being hurt again,
For each time, she was left crying and alone
She wants to hope ... but doesn't trust.
If he wants her heart, he must be patient.

The years of pain melt away and the hurt dissipates,

Suddenly, though it seems impossible,
His touch calms her soul and his words ease her
mind.
So familiar, he just is … what she never knew she
needed – or even wanted.

Looking into his eyes, she sees more than a man,
More than a flickering light or possibility.
She sees all the things she'd always hoped for but
never believed to be possible.
Her truth that was always waiting to be found.

She saw the reflection of her own soul,
A safe harbor for her often careening chaos,
An embrace that would never lack nor turn away.
She saw more than just her future in his eyes.
She saw completion, safety and love.

Through the years of pain and tears,
Heartaches and heartbreak,
What she never knew was missing, she found in
him.
She'd gladly travel all the broken roads again,
To find this place she had discovered.
She had finally come home.

Sometimes

I look over at you beside me and my heart smiles –
I know you love me and care about me,
You want what's best for me and
Never do you want to see me struggle.

But, my dear, there will always be those times ...
When I don't need to be fixed,
I'm not looking for an answer,
Because there's really no problem.
I just need space to clear my head.

I can see the angst in your eyes as you try –
To understand, to stand back, to not help.
But that's just it – I'm really okay.
Sometimes, I just need time for myself.

I can't explain why I need to shut it all out,
Why sometimes the world is just too much,
But know that it isn't and never will be you,
Nor does it mean that I don't love you – I do, more
than you'll ever know.

I know you hate watching, helpless, dear love,
But I promise I'm okay and always will be.
This is just how I recharge, regroup and refocus.
I can't be my best for you if I'm tired inside.
My heart gets weary and my soul becomes listless.

I wish I could explain why I am this way,
But more than that, why you should never worry.

I'll always emerge on the other side,
Brighter, happier and ready to love you with
happiness aglow.

We are two people who found each other against
the odds,
Who've made our uniqueness come together,
And formed a love that will never die.
You're my one truth and love forevermore.

So, as we walk along this path called life together,
Grant me this one wish and be patient –
Understand for me as I will for you,
This is just one of the things I need,
My small times of quiet that help me heal,
As much as I want you, I need this space,
So that I can always be the best me I can be,
And love you exactly the way you'll always deserve
...

'Til we find the place where the horizon meets the
sky,
I'll still be loving you so with all my heart.
Please find a way to try to understand,
Give me this, so I can give you all of me ...
In a way that we will be forever happy,
Together.

Becoming the Fire

She remembered her earliest days as a broken girl
with shattered dreams and never forgot that pain.
Everything she wanted was taken away and
everyone she loved always disappeared.
She learned how to survive at an early age, and she
never forgot those lessons.
She became stronger because she had to be.
She became happier because she learned
independence.
She became smarter because she learned from her
mistakes.
Not because she wanted to, but because she had to.
Every diamond is forged under pressure, and she
found her brilliance through the fiery forges of a hard
life.
Every twist in the road wasn't meant to hurt her, but
to teach her – and she learned.
She clawed, fought and rose stronger from the
ashes.
She stopped asking for an easier path and instead
created an indomitable spirit.
She fell down along the way and lost her spark
sometimes, seemingly quenching the flames of her
heart.
That's when she discovered how to rise again as the
fire, a phoenix reborn.
Passion moved her,
failure taught her,
courage forged her ...
Into a woman that could not and would not be

defeated.

Pain turned her wounds into wisdom and tragedies into triumphs.

She was knocked down often, but she always rose again … stronger and wiser.

She was beautiful in ways that defied reason – she had an incandescent spirit, fiery heart and unconquerable will …

Deep down in her heart and spirit, she would not and could not be denied.

She wasn't eye candy, she was soul food – the sort of person you'd never forget.

She knew what she brought to the table,

And she wasn't afraid to dine alone.

Her scars were a testament to her journey,

And she bore them with proud defiance.

Throw her to the wolves …

And she'd return leading the pack.

Butterfly, lioness, warrior, lover, poet …

This only scratched the surface of who she was.

She learned long ago that a strong woman intimidated boys and excited men.

She didn't need either but knew passion burned brighter in twos.

Call her a flawed person, a beautiful disaster or gorgeous mess, she didn't care.

She lived without labels and loved without regrets, starting with herself.

It wasn't about what or who she had, but who she was.

She didn't need approval or acceptance –

She loved herself, her life and her choices.

She was utterly unforgettable and unique.
She is and always will be more than just
a spark, a light or a flame.
She's a roaring wildfire.
Some women survive the flames ...
She chose to become the fire.

Afraid

I saw it from the very first moment we met.
Your heart was battered and your spirit bruised, but
it was so much more than that.
The last one, the person that you thought was the
one, left your heart in pieces.
They took advantage of you while you just tried to
love them.
They broke your heart, crushed your soul and tried
to break your spirit.
They never really understood you, did they?
For all the promises they made and lies they told,
they still never really got you.
They made you compete for their attention and they
certainly didn't make you feel loved.
You were never really understood, not because you
didn't try to share your heart, but because they didn't
care enough ...
To respect you, to love you or to value you.
They didn't accept or appreciate you for the
wonderful person you'd fought to become.
Now, as I look into your wounded soul, I see tattered
wings that long to fly once more ...
But you're afraid, and I know why.
You don't trust your heart and you certainly don't
trust love ... and why would you?
I don't blame you.
It's the hardest thing to do, isn't it?
To bare your heart and soul, to be vulnerable and
risk the heartbreak all over again.
It's not your fault they never took the time to truly

love you the way you deserve.
It's hard to see your great qualities when your heart is hurting.
But I do know this –
They missed out on the greatest person I've ever met.
You're beautiful in ways that you've not even grasped yet.
You're beautifully broken, and the gorgeous cracks of your wounded soul are simply breathtaking ...
That's how your light gets in, and when you choose to, you shine so beautifully bright.
Don't let the wrong person who didn't love you keep you from the right one who will.
The scars of your heart sing the story of your life, and I admire and cherish every one of your breaks, scratches and scars ...
They make you exactly the beautiful soul I fell in love with.
Truth be told, I'd love to spend the rest of my days loving you in my arms ...
Proving to you that I'll never be like the one or any other that broke your heart.
I know I will need to be patient, but I promise to protect and cherish your heart each and every day.
No matter how long it takes, I've got forever to prove my heart to you, for that's how long I will love you.
I'm unlike any other person that's ever loved you and promised you the world ...
Because I'll be with you 'til the end and beyond, Sharing it all, loving it all, cherishing it all.
That is my word and vow from now until we meet

again in the next life.
I'm ready to build our future, one day at a time.
Can you take that chance with me?

Forgetting Your Heart Was Ever Broken

Never settle for less than you deserve.
Someone, somewhere, is dreaming of a person just like you.
Stop thinking you're so broken that no one will ever want you.
You're exactly what the person meant for you wants and needs.
Expect and demand the very best from anyone who wants to love you –
If they can't give you respect, honesty and communication, then don't give them your heart.
A gentleman will accept your past,
support your present and
encourage your future.
He will hold your hand through the rainy days and celebrate the sunshine beside you.
He'll never treat you like you're his number one – because you'll always be his only one.
True love doesn't settle for being an option and it doesn't require you to sacrifice your self-respect.
Be true to yourself and know what you want.
Be honest with him and expect the same in return.
Love with conviction, live with passion.
Know your worth and own it.
If he's worth having, then he'll know that sometimes, apologizing isn't about right or wrong,
but the importance of the relationship.
Happily ever after doesn't take detours, make

excuses or act disrespectfully.

Take charge of your life and love on your terms, without exception.

Sometimes, life will knock you down, but together, you can weather any storm.

Never stop loving yourself, never stop believing and never stop chasing your dreams.

Fairy tales do come true, but they all start with you.

Decide to fight for what truly matters,

and happiness will always find a way … if you let it.

Choose to embrace life and be open to love and happiness.

In the end, what's meant to be will always find a way if you're receptive.

So often, hearts and minds close the door of opportunity.

It's your life and your choice.

One line at a time, one chapter each day.

Write your story anew and begin to believe that you, too, can have anything you want if you never settle or give up.

If you're going to settle, only settle for the best.

If you're going to give up, only give up your heart to the right one.

If you're going to let go, let go of your past to make way for your future.

Show him your heart … and he'll show you a true and honest love.

He'll be the man that will finally make you forget your heart was ever broken.

Resilient Creatures

Gentlemen, pull up a chair and pay attention.
Respect your lady,
cherish her,
love her when she can't even love herself.
She doesn't always want to talk.
Sometimes, she may just want to lay her head on
your chest and just … be.
That's when she needs you most of all,
Unconditionally and unequivocally.
Truth is, she may not even know why she feels
upside down and inside out –
But she does know that she wants you there,
holding her and making her feel safe.
In those quiet moments when she's still and her
breathing is all you hear …
Soak in the moments.
Those are the memories you'll always cherish.
Just you, her and peace.
Her heart beating against yours.
She may have had a hard day, fought countless
internal battles and even lost it a time or two …
So appreciate that about her.
Her resilience and strength aren't about physical
prowess …
It's the type of emotional courage that would bring
us to our knees.
So, as you caress her hair and feel her resting
heartbeat against you in the still of the night,
Cherish those feelings that only she can give –
They're the most beautiful emotions you'll ever

experience from a magnificent soul ...

Her love.

Her company.

Her affection.

Just ... her.

If you understand that about her, you'll finally realize why she's so amazing.

She's deep, she's loving, she's beautiful ...

But most of all, she's magic.

We Will Always Be My Favorite Love Story

Life isn't always going to have great events and exciting times.

It's those quiet moments we spend together, just the two of us, stolen away from the world that we will truly cherish.

Everyone always says you'll remember the big things – the anniversaries and events, the grand to dos of a life well lived.

But as I look over at you, your hand nestled softy on my arm, I realize those aren't the only feelings that I'll carry in my heart.

It's times like this, the frozen moments that make my soul content as my heart sighs.

Limbs entangled and your beautiful smile illuminating the night, these are the moments that matter most to me.

These are the memories that I'll forever cherish – With you by my side and love in my heart, there is nothing more priceless than being wrapped up in your arms.

So, let's celebrate the fireworks and flash, but always remember it's the time we spend together in the still of the night, quiet and full of love ...

these are the deepest and most heartfelt keepsakes of our life together.

Waking up to see you walk into the room dressed in my oversized dress shirt makes my heart smile in ways I had never dreamt possible.

Thank you for being you … and more than anything,
Thank you for sharing this life and this love with me.
You will always be my baby, my princess, my lady
and greatest triumph.
You showed me a way and a depth that I had never
seen or felt before ...
And now, nothing else makes sense without you.
You're my rhyme, my reason, and my one true thing.
You showed me a life and a love that I never thought
possible.
More than anything, when I'm with you, everything
just makes sense.
I love you ...
More today than yesterday and never as much as I
will tomorrow ...
Always and forever.

Loving Me Just the Way I Am

All my life I've been told what to do, how to look and what I "should be."
They tried to dismiss me, the ones who didn't like the way I walked … talked … carried myself.
If I wasn't like everyone else, then I wasn't acceptable ...
You know what?
That's great with me.
Better to be hated for being authentic than to be loved for being fake.
So many wanted to drag me down because I was different from them.
I've loved, I've lost, I've lived – but I did it all on my terms.
So many times, everyone thought I was finished,
That I was at the end of my rope.
They thought my days numbered and
My choices limited because that's what they wanted.
That couldn't have been further from the truth … my truth.
But the thing is, they never really understood me nor wanted to.
Never underestimate someone who has struggled, stumbled and is still smiling.
I'm more than a survivor, and I'm still standing –
More than that, I'm thriving.
I'm a fighting spirit that can't be vanquished, a soul that can't be broken.
See, that's the thing about people like me – we don't know how to quit.

I'll always get back up, no matter how many times I fall ...
Stronger, wiser and better.
I live hard and I love harder.
Words can't hurt me and deception won't fool me.
I've got a full heart and a lot of love to give someone who gets me.
I don't have the time or patience for empty promises or shallow words.
So, if you want to be part of my life, friend, love or otherwise ... Earn it.
Say what you mean and do what you say.
That's the ethos of who I am, and it's what I deserve ... no, it's what I demand.
Respect, honor, strength, heart – it's ingrained in parts of me that I can't describe.
Save the lukewarm passion and lighthearted courage, that's not what I want in love or life.
So, if you're ready to stand up and stand strong,
I'll be right here, shining brighter than ever,
Waiting to love and respect you.
I've got a big heart and a tougher skin.
I'm a lover.
I'm a fighter.
I'm a dreamer.
Love me or leave me, I'm okay with not being everyone's taste.
But can you accept me, with all my flaws and mistakes, my scars and baggage ... without trying to change me?
I love me just the way I am.
The question is ... can you?

The Beauty of Vulnerability

All his life, they told him he had to be strong.
He was told to repress his feelings and guard who he truly was.
He yearned to release his emotions that he locked away behind high walls, but they called that weak.
To give into his soul and show the world his truth would be his undoing ... or so he thought.
He fought for the courage to be brave – not for the strength to overcome, but from letting his feelings overwhelm the walls around his heart.
All that he knew and was told to be wasn't who he was meant to become.
He soon learned that the hardest challenge was showing the woman he loved the true depth of his soul.
He lacked the words and often the tenacity to let his feelings pour forth.
He yearned to understand her, to share all of himself with her on a level that scared him.
Only when he was heart to heart with her did he begin to understand the true depths of real and meaningful love.
She loved his strength but, more than anything, she embraced his vulnerability.
His ability to convey his hopes, dreams and fears were what she had loved most.
Slowly, he began to reveal more of his soul and the raw emotions that she cherished.
Finally, when he had thrown off his guarded mantle and became what he wanted to be ...

That's when he finally understood what it meant to be a strong man.
It was never about being able to withstand the storms or fighting back the feelings.
Truly loving himself and sharing his soul was the hardest battle he'd ever faced.
For his happiness, her love and a dream fulfilled, he faced the fire he once feared would consume him ...
He emerged stronger, wiser and able to truly love her in the ways she longed for and deserved.
It was in those moments that he discovered his truths ...
They were real, they were raw, but they were always authentic.
And for the rest of his days, he wouldn't have it any other way.
She loved him for who he was, how he loved her and most of all, how he shared himself with her ... completely.
He no longer wanted to be hard or heroic ... more than anything,
He just wanted to be hers.

I Hope Your Coffee Tastes Like Magic

I hope today is the day that you start to feel alive again ...

Where beauty is all around you, and you feel like you can do anything.

That the smell of freshly brewed coffee and a vibrant sunrise energizes your spirit anew.

When the laughter of small children makes you smile, the smell of flowers fills your heart and wet puppy kisses make you laugh.

Let today be the day when you discover a new adventure, take that chance to be happy and invigorate your soul again.

I hope that the sunlight warms your heart and that a long-lost friend finds you once more.

I hope your dreams feel so real you can touch them, and all the worries and cares you have just melt away.

I hope that the magic you somehow lost along the way finds you again and you start to believe in yourself, your heart and better days ahead.

I hope you remember all the things you love, uncover new things that enchant your mind, and start chasing your dreams again.

I hope that you never stop believing in love and know that it will come for you when the time is right ... And if you've already found it, then may your passions, love and desire burn brighter, feel stronger and find the butterflies once more.

Where the stars inspire you, the ocean grants you serenity, and you find your joy in the small things you may have once overlooked.

I know that with love in your heart, passion in your soul and life in your spirit,

You can fly higher than you ever dreamed.

I hope that today, the sky is a little bit brighter, the music is a little bit happier and the sunset is a little bit more beautiful.

I hope that today, you fall in love with being alive again.

That is my wish for you ...

Today and for always.

Limited Only by Imagination

When it comes to her,
Don't try to limit who she is,
Who she wants to become,
What she is capable of achieving.
Embrace her individuality and her passions,
Run beside her as she chases her dreams.
Understand that she's not perfect,
But it's that gritty imperfection that makes her just
who she is –
A lover, a dreamer, a lady, a partner ...
A fighter, a soulmate, a survivor.
If you accept her for all her flaws,
See her for the beautiful woman she has worked
hard to become,
She'll love you in ways you've never experienced:
Faithfully, passionately, soulfully and sensually.
Love her for the magnificent person that she is,
Protect her as the delicate heart she has,
Care for her as the soulmate that she is,
And walk with her for the companion that she will
always be.
Listen to her desires, her fears, the whispers from
her darkest places.
Love her completely, without judgment and
condition, each and every day.
Know that to love her is
To understand her ...
To appreciate her ...
To crave her ...
To respect her ...

And then you'll finally begin to see the vision of her true nature.
She's a versatile creature of multiple talents, personas and abilities.
She's more than a woman, a lady or a lover.
She's the love of your life and the fire for your heart.
Hold on tightly to those glimpses into the beautiful soul of her,
For in those moments,
You'll finally begin to understand who she really is,
And you'll realize the wonder of a woman:
She's magical, she's one of a kind, and most of all,
She's all yours.

A Hundred Years

I never meant to fall in love with you,
it just happened.
You smiled and stole my heart before I realized I
had fallen for you.
I never really stood a chance, but then, I really didn't
want to.
You blew in like a whirlwind and ripped my defenses
asunder, and I was yours – with a beautiful smile
and a sumptuous kiss.
Loving you wasn't even an option, because when
your soul called to mine across a windswept plane, I
fell completely head over heels for you.
Your words careened across my skin with
precocious splendor,
And your lips upon mine seduced me with a fiery
passion that I have never known.
As the days have passed and our hearts have
begun to beat as one,
I realized more and more how very familiar you've
always been to me.
We were never strangers even at the moment we
met,
We just hadn't found each other yet in this lifetime.
I knew when I looked in your eyes that our love was
timeless – without beginning or end.
Mate of my soul, you have been my twin flame since
before the chapters of time ever turned the first
page.
Head to heart to spirit to soul, we've loved each
other across countless times and endless places.

Against impossible odds, we've always found our way back to each other's arms.
Our love has endured when all else failed,
your touch has always electrified my senses and calmed my restless spirit.
More than just butterflies and sweet whispers,
You've been my reason for being and my light in the darkness.
I'll hold your hand in mine as we face the world and years together,
And I'll find you once more in the next life ...
Even if I have to wait a hundred years to love you again,
I'd count the minutes until you are there, waiting for me –
Knowing that my forever begins and ends ...
With you.
I'd gladly wait for a hundred years if it meant you were waiting for me at the end.
Each and every time.
That's love.
That's true.
That's us.
We are and always will be forever.

The Start of Something Beautiful

Yes, I got knocked down.
Truth is, I didn't know if I could get back up ...
And I didn't even think I wanted to.
Then, I remembered who I am and what I'm capable of.
I'm a survivor.
I'm a fighter.
I'm a dreamer.
I've survived the worst of life, and I've fought for everything I am.
I believe in the power of my dreams, and I'll not rest until I catch them.
I'd rather have five great friends than a hundred fake ones.
I keep my circle tight and my heart guarded because I know my worth, and I don't just share it with anyone.
I'm there for anyone I love, and I expect the same in return.
I don't want a lover, one night or lukewarm love.
I deserve and crave much more than that.
I'm holding out for passion, soul love and an authentic partnership.
I don't need someone in my life, and I love myself completely,
So anyone who wants to be in my life should be all the things that matter.
Respectful.
Loyal.
Real.

People may call me feisty, snobbish or sassy, but that's just because they don't try to understand me. My life, my love, my way, my style.

I don't seek approval and I don't ask for permission. I stand in my own light, and I don't need to put out another's fire to burn brightly.

There's a lot of days that I don't want to get out of bed, and even more that I can't get out of my own head.

But, see, that's just the thing about me.

I own my beautiful chaos and know I'm a mess sometimes.

That doesn't take away from the wonderful person I've fought to become.

I'm real, I'm authentic and I'm always going to love hard when there's love to be had.

Rain or shine, rise or fall, I'll always keep my head, standards and heels high.

I don't have time for anyone's possibly, maybe or sometimes.

It's taken me a long time to learn to love myself the way I should, and I'm not going to sacrifice that for anyone who doesn't see me for who I am.

Sometimes?

I'm unsure, I'm stressed and I'm worried.

But I'm also ...

Bold, confident and passionate.

So, If you can get on board with me and all my glorious disaster, then let's go chase some adventure.

Love me for me, give what you get and respect who I am.

That's all I ask.

I'll always be my very best for you, every time.

Can you do the same?

I Won't Lose Who I Am to Become What You Want

When you decided I wasn't the one for you anymore,
You helped me realize a few things about myself
that I guess I never knew.
Sure, I'd been battered, bruised and broken and
thought I'd lost my way completely, but I hoped I
always had you in my corner.
Turns out, you weren't in this for me after all.
Truth is, I had started to lose who I was trying to
make you happy.
They say sometimes love just isn't enough ...
This is one of those times.
You wanted me to be what you wanted, on your
terms, in your way.
In your mind, you had this picture of who and what
you thought I should be ...
Your happiness mattered more than mine, and it
always would.
I thought I could change to make you happy, but I
lost myself in the process.
Did you ever really love me for me?
Or was it just what I embodied and what I
represented?
Did you ever really see me for who I am?
When you saw that I was strong enough to stand up
for who I was and wouldn't give into your selfish
requests ... You decided that you'd had enough.
Getting what you want meant more than supporting
and loving me in the way I deserved – for who I truly

was.

Now that I'm walking out of your life, I can't help but cry inside.

Cry for what I thought we had.

Cry for what we could have been.

Cry for the love that I wish was real.

Maybe you loved me in your own way, hoping that I would change to be everything you wanted me to be ... But that's just it.

Love is acceptance.

Love is understanding.

Love is true.

Asking me to change who I am to be what you want isn't love at all.

I'm just glad I saw the truth before I lost myself trying to please you.

I'll never forget the times we had and the smiles we shared, but you gave me the greatest gift of all, and I'm thankful for that reason.

You showed me that I'm good enough to be loved on my terms for all my flaws and uniqueness.

Nothing and no one will ever change my self-worth because I won't let that happen.

My jagged edges and imperfect flaws are just the things that make me beautiful.

You didn't appreciate that about me, but someone will. That's where I'll find my happily ever after.

Loving another imperfect person perfectly.

Some people were meant to be in your heart, not your life.

I'm holding out for the one who deserves to be in both.

A Million Things I Don't Say

I'm the one that you always think is happy.
Always smiling, ever laughing ...
I'm the picture of joy and happiness –
Or so you think.
Behind my eyes are countless truths that most will
never know because they just won't understand ...
Nor do they try to.
They think a pretty smile and free spirit are enough
to make anyone happy, and I'm good with that.
Truth is, I often cry myself to sleep, arguing with the
demons that I have to dance with for just the briefest
respite from all the thoughts.
Everyone would just tell me I'm lonely and to just go
socialize.
It's not that simple.
Sure, I'm lonely sometimes, most of the time by
choice.
I love my friends and enjoy my times with them, but
sometimes you can feel completely alone in a room
full of people.
I don't chase fake friends with my real dreams and
expect them to get it.
My hopes, my dreams, my fears ... they're both a
blessing and a curse.
I've long since made peace with my broken journey
and found solace in picking up my pieces along the
way.
I find my joy in the little things and treasure every ray
of sunshine that I come across ...
But, when the night comes, I realize I need more

than that.

I just want someone to understand, accept and love me.

I know I'm not the easiest nor simplest soul out there, but my heart is always aglow and my soul and my spirit are fiery.

I don't expect miracles, and I don't need to be saved, but I do demand respect, love and courtesy … among other things.

I'm tired of nursing a glass of wine to sleep and need so much more than a regular life.

I was meant to chase the passions that set my soul on fire.

Sure, I'll always smile and be the life of the party, but when the music stops, the silence can become deafening.

I want out of my head and into my dreams.

I feel so often like I'm losing my mind or that I'm just sorta strange in my own way ...

And I'm okay with that.

I love like a wildfire and live without expectations.

I don't make apologies and I have no regrets ...

Save one.

That behind the walls that protect my heart, I'm alone.

Granted, by choice, but alone isn't about how or why.

Every day, when I see the dawn break on a new day, I feel the stirring of hope.

Maybe today won't be like the rest.

Perhaps today I can finally find my own ray of sunshine and tuck it away into my soul for later.

Maybe today, someone will come along and say all the right things, see me for who I truly am, and most of all,
Understand all the things that I have yet to say that are hidden behind my eyes ...
Because they already know my soul.
Until then, I'll keep smiling and hoping.
Sometimes, you just need a lot of love and a little magic.
I'll never stop believing and let destiny do the rest.
That's how dreams are born ...
Starting with me.

A Gentleman Will Make Her Feel Like a Goddess

Where has the romance gone?
Has the valiant pursuit of courting a woman gone by the wayside?
Have men forgotten how to treat a lady?
While I know that this doesn't apply to all men, take heed, those who may be in need of a refresher.
Chivalry may not be lost, but gentlemen, here are some ideas about how to truly romance a lady.
Catch her eye with your style and charm,
But engage her mind to further the conversation.
Don't try to impress her with fancy gadgets and try to buy her affection.
Any good woman will be more attracted to your character and manners than to any amount of superficiality.
Sure, the big things matter ... but the details do too:

- Plan the date but find out what she likes.
- First ... listen, listen, listen.
- No lady wants to hear a monologue about your life.
- Dates and relationships are conversations, not speeches.
- Be interested: in who she is, wants she wants and her dreams.
- Share your thoughts, hopes and desires – don't be afraid to be real and vulnerable. Any woman worth having will love those ideals.

- If you want to speak to her heart, start with her head.
- Treat her with respect.
- Fulfill your promises.
- Be honest, authentic and willing to try to understand her.
- Remember that the little things also matter, just as much.
- Surprise her with love notes.
- Take her to her favorite café.
- Open her door, take her coat, pull out her chair.
- Hold her hand and flirt with her.

Oh, and women love it if you play with their hair … in any fashion.

Engage her mind, emblazon her heart and set her passions on fire.

Be a man of quality if you seek a lady of dignity … and that's a two-way street.

Let's resurrect the traditions of generations past. Court your ladies, win their hearts and make them feel special.

If you want just anyone, keep doing what you're doing.

If you want a once in a lifetime lady, then do whatever it takes,

But do it all ... like a gentleman.

Soul Food

A little girl once made a promise to herself that she vowed to never forget:
She would always chase her dreams,
While remaining true to herself.
That same little girl became an amazing woman, successful and independent.
The difference between her and all the rest?
She didn't sell her soul to make it to the top.
She fought, clawed and sacrificed every step of the way and earned everything she achieved.
She wasn't just a pretty face, she was a beautiful soul with a fierce heart.
Anyone that underestimated her discovered their mistake quickly.
The most amazing part of this strong woman?
She kept that little girl's promise.
She lifted up the others that no one would even acknowledge.
She picked up the fallen and carried them until they could carry themselves.
She would fix the crown of another without telling the world it was crooked.
Never forgotten were her beginnings,
Never lost was her vow made so long ago.
Those who crossed her path could only wonder what it was that made this woman so soulfully beautiful.
That intangible quality that defied description was her depth that most would fail to understand ...
The passion of her heart,
The radiance of her soul,

The courage of her spirit.
If you ever met her,
And truly saw her for the person she was,
That's when you realized what others sometimes missed.
She was beautiful, not for her makeup, hair or style,
But for all the things that truly matter.
Heart. Character. Love. Passion.
She'd leave an impression on you,
Not on your eyes, but somewhere so much deeper.
Her unique way of touching your depths was most remarkable and indescribable.
She didn't need a spotlight,
She shone from within.
After all, she was so much more than eye candy ...
She was soul food.

I'll Never Be Your Maybe

Honey,

I'm not the kind of person that will wait for you to "figure things out."

I know what I want and who I want it from – I expect the same from you.

If you can't make me a priority, then don't think that I'll stick around as a possibility.

I know my worth and I'm as good as they come.

If you can't see that, someone else will.

I may not have everything always figured out and I may just have "those" days. Sometimes I cry in the shower, but then, who doesn't?

I never said I was perfect, and I don't ever want to be.

So, if you're looking for Barbie, Ken, you won't find her here.

I'm imperfectly beautiful in all the most chaotically wonderful ways, and if you'd stop looking at me and start actually seeing me, you might just get that.

I need someone strong, confident and passionate –
I don't want to sit idly and watch a small camp fire, I want passion fiery enough to set a thousand nights ablaze.

If you're trying to define me like every other woman you've known, then let me just stop you right there.

You may never figure me out, you might have a challenge trying to understand me, but if you want something badly enough, I'd think you'd do your best to try to unravel my layers.

True love and blazing romance doesn't just appear

for the faint of heart.

You can call me stubborn, headstrong or sassy – I'll just smile and thank you for the compliments.

I'm not going to be just another option in your playbook, and I'm not happy settling for small slivers of your attention.

So, this is your chance, and I'm your wake up call.

If you're playing a game, then find another field to play on.

My love isn't something I take lightly, and I don't waste my time with hopscotch of the heart.

So, do us both a favor, won't you?

Forget your maybes, hopefully and possibilities.

Step up and treat me with respect if you want to earn my love.

My life isn't a dress rehearsal, and this isn't an audition.

This time … I'm playing for keeps.

Love Her So Much that She May Doubt Your Sanity … but Never Your Passion

Before you came into my life,
I would never have believed there was a good kind
of crazy – until you showed me differently.
You turned everything upside down and changed all
the things I thought I knew about myself, life and
love.
You made everything finally make sense in a way
that I never knew was possible.
The wish I made for true love so long ago came true
in you.
You drive me crazy – but in the best way,
and I wouldn't trade that for anything.
If my passion-infused devotion and lovingly-intense
desire for you puts me on the edge just a bit …
then I will gladly walk that line to spend a lifetime in
your arms.
Call me crazy,
Call me passionate,
Call me intense,
Just so long as you always
Call me yours.

Your Most Fierce Days

I'm not always sunshine and rainbows, just the opposite some days.
It's those days when I have thunderstorms and lightning behind my eyes that I'm at my honest truth.
The days when all I want to do is curl up in a corner and cry … but I face the world anyways.
Everyone always wants to share in the happy days, but there's bad times mixed in and always will be.
I fight through the hard days and, somehow, find a way to force a smile for the world.
Give me the people that will stand beside me at my lowest.
Find me the ones that will love and accept me at my worst.
Show me a partner that may not always understand me but will always listen and care.
I know I'm not the easiest person to love nor am I always easy to understand, but I'm loyal to a fault and I'm real to my core.
I speak the truth when others don't and I hold myself to a standard that doesn't make excuses or settle.
So, if you want to know me for who I really am, don't come looking for me when I'm happy.
Do just the opposite.
Seek me out on the dark days when I'm struggling and fighting for my smile.
I'm a fiercely passionate and a courageous chaos that does more than survives ... I thrive.
I'm not wired to be anything other than real, authentic and passionate, and I'm a splendid mess

even when I can't help it.

So, love me for who I am and accept me for what I'm not, but either way, you know you'll always get the truth and an undying love and loyalty.

I'm fierce, I'm passionate and most of all, I'm a dreamer.

I do more than exist, I'm alive and chasing my dreams with a zealous heart.

You may not always get me, but you'll always get my best,

This I promise you ...

On my worst days and my best, you'll know where you stand and what I need from you.

If you're going to be in my life – friend, partner or confidant,

Don't be anything other than kind, compassionate or positive ...

Because that's who I am and always will be.

In the end, you may not understand why I'm a beautiful disaster or delightful mystery, only that I'm one of a kind.

The look in my eyes is unmistakable and the fire in my heart undeniable ...

Dig deep into my soul –

You'll finally see in my eyes everything you never knew you wanted ... until I showed you why you did.

Can you get onboard with that?

I Am Confident, I Am Beautiful, I Am Enough

My story hasn't always been a tale of easy days and triumphant victory.
There's been a lot of chapters of struggle, failure and loss.
But through it all, I've remained true to who I am and what I want.
I turned every setback into a comeback and every closed door into a new chance.
I'm really a deep person who enjoys quiet times and simple things –
I always need those serene moments to reflect, recharge and rebound.
I've had my heart broken more times than I can remember and been cast aside more than anyone should be.
I learned from every broken road and evolved after each dead-end relationship.
I realized along the way what was most important – totally loving myself for who I am.
I'm too much for some people, but it takes a strong person to appreciate a fiery heart.
I'll never be lukewarm in my passion, and I'll always love my people hard when there's love to be had.
I had to accept that some days I'll want to cry in the shower and scream at the toaster, but that's okay –
I'll always be real and authentic.
I'll take a deep soul with beautiful chaos every day over merely existing.

I may fall, I may stumble, I may fail ...
But it will always be on my terms.
Each and every day, I look in the mirror and remember where I've been and the fires that forged my survivor spirit.
That's when I smile deeply because I know:
I am confident.
I am beautiful.
And I will always be ...
More than enough.

Hold My Hand and Don't Ever Let Me Go

I can't always promise days without storms,
Or nights without darkness.
But I can promise you won't have to face them
alone,
My hand in yours,
Our hearts beating as one,
My home in your arms,
My love forever in your eyes.
In those moments of weakness,
When the world has gotten you down,
And life has taken its toll,
Take my hand in yours,
Meet my gaze with your eyes,
And hold fast to one truth:
I'll always be there, by your side, to weather any
storm.
You're never alone, my love …
And you never will be again.
Hold my heart in yours,
Ours souls united ...
And always know that we can overcome anything,
Together,
You and I as one ...
Forever.

A Love for the Ages

Darlin',
I know that you're afraid of so many things –
To be hurt again,
to be lied to by another,
to be abandoned once more.
Most of all, to fall for someone who isn't willing to
catch you.
I'm afraid too, you know.
I'm afraid to have finally have found a beautiful but
scared soul ...
but to fail to bring you back –
To glimpse your soul across your walls but not be
able to find you midst the pain.
I have my doubts and wonder if I'm the one who can
be all you need,
If I'm strong enough to help us both ...
To trust again.
To hope again.
To believe again.
Most of all, to love again.
I fear losing the chance to love the most amazing
person I have ever met.
Times won't always be perfect and they won't always
be easy,
but come what may,
I promise to face them all by your side.
So, if you don't see all the wonderful parts of
yourself that I appreciate,
if the thought of love scares you as it may,
then take my hand and we will stand together,

strong and faithful until time is no more.
With love in our hearts and courage in our spirits, we
can conquer anything that comes our way ...
So long as we do it together.
I can't stop the rainy days nor make the sun shine,
but my arms can be your shelter from any storm ...
a love for the ages,
And an embrace to protect you as you've never
known.
Respect, love, empathy and passion – a beginning
to our healing journey.
I hold out my hand and open my heart, hoping,
loving and believing –
in you, me and us.
One love, one hope and one dream of forever.
Will you take my hand ...
And give me that chance?

Strong

While all the other girls were playing with dolls, I was focused on building a better me.

I never asked for an easier life, I asked for a stronger will.

My life has never been sunshine and roses, but I wouldn't have it any other way.

I've survived the hard times and evolved with every stumble, fall and mistake.

I learned to rise from the ashes of my failures and become stronger with each conquered mountain.

There's still days when I don't want to get out of bed and I feel like my to do list is longer than my patience, but that's just part of life.

You can either dwell in the hardship or rise to the challenge.

I prefer to take my stumbling stones and build a path to my success.

I'm real, authentic and chase my dreams with an unwavering passion.

I have what matters most to me:

A kind spirit, fierce heart and an old soul.

I know who I am and my worth, and I'll accept nothing less from my life, my friends or my partner.

The fire in my heart and depth in my soul means that not everyone will understand me, but I'm okay with that.

I won't always be everyone's cup of tea, but I'll always be an original.

It's better to be hated for your uniqueness than to be loved for being fake.

I've got a lot of love to give, and I know what I want.
I'll always be ride or die for my people, and I'll do anything for those I love.
I don't have time for people who treat me like an option when I make them a priority.
Some may say I have an attitude, but I call that having standards.
Forget the small talk and meaningless things, I want substance, heart and adventures that fill my soul.
I'll never have to ask myself "why didn't I?" –
because I'll take the chance and try the things that once scared me.
I'll follow my heart but always take my head with me.
You'll always know where I stand and what I want ...
Can you roll with that?

Her Eyes Will Tell You Everything that She Has Yet to Say

Behind the most beautiful eyes lay secrets deeper
than the darkest night.
They are the most powerful tools a woman has –
she can seduce you,
Reduce you or
even refuse you,
But you'll never forget the look in her eyes.
It's the window to all that she is,
her heart and the beauty that lies within.
Her eyes can captivate you,
not because of the color,
but because of all the unspoken words they contain.
She doesn't need to say a word and quiet speaks
volumes for what she thinks,
Everything she feels.
When you gaze into her fire, there's no lie there.
If you can discern the emotions that lay hidden
beyond the panes of her soul, you'll begin to
discover the wondrous beauty of a woman.
She'll yearn for you,
She'll burn for you,
But most of all, she'll always return for you ...
If you've proven that you can love, respect and
appreciate her the way she deserves.
With one look, she can turn a man inside out and tell
her story without a single whisper.
Stop and breathe in her unspoken visual language,
For she has an intense love and an even greater

passion ...
But it all starts in those beautiful eyes.
If you truly wish to uncover the mystery of who a woman is,
start there, in her eyes ...
Her spirit, her heart, her soul.
She might be a beautiful disaster and an amazing mess,
The wild-heart wanderlust that won't be tamed,
But she'll change your whole world with just one look.
When you find her, don't hesitate, else she might vanish in an instant.
Take her in your arms, love her intensely and always appreciate her for all that she is ...
But whatever you do, when you happen upon the most wonderful love you've ever known,
Look in her eyes, hold her heart and
Don't ever let her go.

When He Gazes with His Heart

The wonderful thing about that handsome man
across the room?
He was the answer to all the questions she never
knew how to ask.
He showed up suddenly, without a warning, and
stole away her heart.
She didn't know how or when she had slowly taken
down the walls around her heart, but for him … she
had.
Truth be told, she couldn't be happier falling in love
with the grizzled man who walked softly but had that
certain je ne sais quoi.
She couldn't quite place her finger on what it was,
but people just gravitated to him ... and she was no
exception.
When she fell, and she had, she did so hard – she
always did ...
She'd been burned before, but there was something
comforting about this stolid man whose calm
demeanor reassured her amidst her worst doubting.
He knew how to read her and did so effortlessly ...
He knew what to say and how to say it, and there
were so many times that she was left speechless.
She was normally the logical and elusive one, who
used rationale and reason to talk her way out of
emotions like love and desire.
Nonsense, she thought.
She had no time for the emotional upheaval of love
that just didn't make sense ...
Until him.

She wanted to fight it – and she tried with all her might ... to no avail.

What amazed her most about this man who found the way to reach her soul as no one before him had ever dreamt ... was in his gaze.

Across the room, she would be curled up with a book and look up to find him watching her and smiling.

He looked at her with a thoughtful gaze, a warm and sensitive way that somehow comforted her.

Because she knew, beyond all else, he saw her ... truly understood her for who she was.

He looked past her eyes and could calm her mind with nothing more than a solitary glance.

As she smiled, the twinkle in her eye sparked a warm grin in his calm countenance.

They hadn't spoken a word, but in those moments across the room, they had a conversation of the depth that warmed her heart.

That's when she knew.

He was the one that she would love for always, not for what he said, but what never had to be said between them.

Kindred spirits are just that.

Meant to be.

Try as she might, she couldn't deny the truth –
She saw in him the love that she felt and the feelings that she knew were about to explode.

There's a time to fight, a time to run ... and then there was the place she had found –
A time to believe in something more.
Him. Her.

Love.
She knew that this was a moment she'd remember for the rest of her life ...
When she knew he was her forever.

True Love is Worth the Wait

I choose you and always will, from the first time I
ever saw you to my last breaths that leave this life.
Every single day, through the happiness and the
tears, I will always choose you –
to have and to hold,
to face all of life's challenges and victories,
to celebrate our life and our love ...
These are only a few of the many things that I
choose, with you, for you and because of you.
They say that life is a series of choices made, and
that may well be true,
but every closed door and failed love led me to your
arms.
I'd say that I'd choose to go back and take away all
the pain that the past caused you, but then the hurt
and the angst only made you into the beautifully
broken and wonderfully strong person that I love
today.
I choose to share our moments, both big and small,
to make the memories that will leave our hearts full
and our souls content.
It seemed like an eternity waiting for you – and I
always knew you were right around a corner
someday, so I fought to always believe and never
lose hope in you, in me, in us.
I choose you to build a life with, chase dreams
beside and love forevermore, for that is our blessing
that I will always cherish, never doubt and ever be
thankful for.
As much as I'd like to say that I chose you all along,

our love story was written in the stars long before our souls ever reunited.

Meant to be, happily ever after, all the phrases that couples utter doesn't begin to tell our tale of two souls that found a way to each other despite the distance, the odds and the broken roads that threatened to tear us apart.

So, as I take your face in my hands and drink in your soulful eyes, know that you gave me hope when I had little, purpose when I searched for mine, and a love that has shown me the happiness that I never knew was possible.

I choose you, every day, in every way, to fall in love with all over again.

I choose to give you my heart, mind and soul as I always have, until the end of days.

It's a choice that is and always will be the foundation of the life we built together, the dreams we share and the love affair that never ends.

Our love story.

No matter how long I may have waited to find you, I'd wait countless lifetimes again to have the chance to love you once more.

I love you.

I Don't Need to Be Saved … I Need to Be Seen

I know you're used to being the shining knight who rescues the damsel in distress,
But I'm not a gal who needs to be found, saved or fixed.
I'll always speak my mind and stand in my own light, because that's just how I'm wired.
You'll always know where you stand with me, because I don't mince words and I always make good on my promises.
There's days when I sparkle and shine, but there's even more times when I rise and grind.
I'm not always put together nor do I always have things under control –
In fact most of the time you can count on me to be a beautiful mess and not even know what day it is.
I don't seek approval nor do I want permission.
I am who I am, unapologetically and without expectation.
Yes, I'm strong-willed, brave when I have to be and fiercely independent ...
But I'm also compassionately kind and lovingly loyal.
I don't turn my back on my people, and I love very deeply.
If you want to be part of my life, step to my standards, don't expect me to lower my expectations.
I'm worth every bit of what I want, and anyone that can't handle that can see themselves out.

Just because I'm smiling doesn't mean I'm not crying inside – I have days just like everyone else ...
I've just learned how to put on a happy face.
I know what I want and where I'm going, so if you can walk beside me and give me your best every day,
Then let's go find some love, passion and adventure.
Every day may not be a victory, but I'll handle it all with grace and charm.
After all, even Cinderella didn't ask for a prince –
She just wanted a night off and some killer shoes ... the rest just fell into place.
So, no, I don't have a plan, and I don't have a clue what tomorrow will bring,
But if you can bring your A game, respect and love me like I deserve,
Then take my hand in yours and let's go chase some dreams together.
After all, happiness is better when shared with the ones you love.

Magic in the Moments

On the days when life tries to sweep me away, those are the times when I steal away and find a hidden corner.

Whether it's the solitude of a peaceful terrace or the quietness of a table tucked away at a cafe, I seek out the beauty in each day.

From hectic mornings to eventful evenings, I often get caught up in the bustle of a busy life, as do we all.

But that's when I make the effort to find the little joys nestled in the beautiful moments of a day that I might have otherwise missed.

Whether it's the laughter of a small child, the aroma of a freshly brewed coffee, the smile of a kind stranger or just the soothing appeal of an isolated patio seemingly waiting for me, I soak in those opportunities to cherish this life I have.

I close my eyes, remember my blessings and simply enjoy the serene chance I have to appreciate where I am, who I've become and the life I've built.

Surely, I have challenges and hard days, but my joy will always trump my troubles ... because I choose that mindset.

I choose to appreciate the beautiful stars under a tranquil night, to love the radiating light of a fresh dawn sun.

I choose to remind you every day, in every way, just why I love you so very much.

I choose to take an instant and just look at the person that's changed my life and filled my heart with love.

I choose to laugh often, live courageously and love passionately.

Those truths don't just find you midst the events of the day, you have to acknowledge them.

No, I stop, take a deep breath and let the wonderful moments of my life refill my soul.

So, whether it's a gracious compliment, random act of kindness or just appreciating the life and love I've been so fortunate to have found, I do more than just recognize those moments of sunlight sprinkled across my days and nights.

Those are the little pockets of reflection that I'll always hold onto and linger in for as long as I possibly can.

As I sit quietly and reminisce, I cherish those chances to enjoy the love I have, the person I've become and the happiness I've created.

My heart is full in those moments, and my soul is shining its brightest.

And those are the memories that will last a lifetime – For me, for you, for us.

That's when I remember and smile:

Sometimes, it's the little things that end up being the big things after all.

Life isn't measured by the breaths we take, but indeed, but the moments that take our breath away.

I'll take a lifetime of breathless moments, little things and endless smiles, so long as you're by my side.

Here's to sunrise snuggles, candlelight eats, hand holding for no reason and simply living in the moments.

That's where the magic is ...
With you, for you and most of all,
Because of you.
You helped me finally understand ...
How it feels to be truly alive.

Rising from the Ashes

Yes, I went down the wrong roads and made all the
bad choices,
I ended up in places I never should have been in
ways that tore my spirit apart.
Truth be told, I don't know how I got so down and
out,
Nor how I made it out intact and still whole.
At the end of my rope and hating who I'd become,
I hit rock bottom.
Everyone counted me out and no one gave me a
chance ...
Even I didn't know how to dig myself out of the hole
... But you know,
That's the thing about a spirit that won't give up.
I don't know how to quit, and I'm meant to become
more in spite of my rough start.
It was never meant to be the end of my story, I just
had to begin a new chapter – one where the
Phoenix rises from the ashes.
I pulled myself up, dusted myself off then fought and
clawed my way back.
I didn't ask for help and no one offered me a hand,
but that was what I needed to forge my own courage
and build my own strength.
My dreams didn't have an expiration, and I wasn't
going to quit on them or myself.
I know I'm a mess sometimes,
A bit of a broken soul with glimpses of beauty
stashed in between,
But I'm good with that.

I made my way, earned my place, and I'm fighting to make my story a success.

I've got a lot of love to give and a passionate fire that can't be quenched.

Sometimes, you realize along the way that you don't set out to be strong and courageous,

But when you're left holding the pieces of a life gone wrong,

Those are the only choices you have left.

It's not that I'll never be beautiful, strong and amazing like the stories of heroes and lovers,

But at least I'll write my story my way, and that's what matters most of all.

I don't have to set the world on fire, just be on fire for my life –

The kind of flames that make your heart and soul feel totally alive.

I may be beautifully broken and wonderfully imperfect,

But I'm still standing.

I'm still strong.

I figured out where I needed to go and what it would take to get there, so I made a choice:

I'm not going looking for a hero,

I've decided to become the hero of my own story

One small victory at a time ... my way.

Kiss Her Every Time Like It's the First

Gentlemen:
If you're going to kiss your lady, do more than just press your lips against hers.
A kiss is a meaningful expression of how you feel about her – make it mean something.
Kiss her in such a way that she'll never forget it, each and every time.
Don't rush in and waste one of those special chances to express your love in a kiss.
Pour your heart into those moments when your lips meet,
So that she'll crave the next encounter.
Brush her hair out of her face,
Cradle her cheek in your hand,
Look intently into her eyes,
Don't just kiss.
Ignite your souls with passion.
Soft, but forceful,
Gentle, but deeply.
Sweet, but strong.
Do more than just kiss her lips,
Leave her breathless.
Playful bites in between the blissful embrace,
Become the wolf before the hunt.
Show her that she's about to be devoured.
Linger but for a moment,
Until her eyes flutter to match her heart.
Your lips brush slightly against hers,
The deep breath before the plunge.
Use your kiss to say all the things that you've

wanted to express –
Kiss her every time like it's your first ... and last.
If you can consume her soul with the passion and
desire that you feel for her,
Then she'll be yours forever.
That is when you'll finally understand ...
How it feels to be truly alive.
It is in those moments when your lips collide
That you want her heart to hunger for you,
Insatiably, intensely, longingly.
She'll never forget how much she wants, loves and
needs you ...
You just have to give her the reason.
Be the reason, with your heart, in that kiss, and
she'll love you and want you ...
Forevermore.

Behind My Smile

I know you've been hurt,
you've cried endless tears,
and you've been broken in ways that you can't even
explain.
You've always wiped away the anguish, found your
smile and laughed again somehow.
Your ability to smile through the tears makes you
that much more beautiful.
You've always found a way to rise from the ashes of
a broken heart.
Try as they might, they could never clip your wings.
Those tears that rolled down your ivory cheeks …
they weren't for you, were they?
You wept for them, as you knew they were lost more
than you ever have been.
They didn't deserve you on their best day and you
didn't deserve that on your worst.
Courage with charisma.
Strength with class.
You embodied all the ideals that no one quite ever
understood about you.
They couldn't get past the smiles and laughter,
The woman they thought they knew … but didn't at
all.
You played your part and played it well, assembling
a convincing facade for the world to see.
You did it to protect your heart and stay strong for
everyone else,
Because that's just who you are.
There's no need to hide your truth from me, for I see

past the pain,
Through the thinly veiled wall of angst
And the storm clouds that protect your soul.
You've fought to become who you are, and it's a marvelous tribute to your courage, dignity and inner beauty.
You've never looked back, but sometimes, I know the loneliness can be overwhelming.
Sometimes, you stop laughing because you're just trying to survive.
The night may be beautiful, but in the silence of twilight is a deafening silence of worries, thoughts.
I see you.
I feel your soul.
Not for the woman you want the world to see, but for the magnificent person that you are.
I know you thought for so long that you would never find someone ...
And you didn't.
I saw you first.
I haven't been the same since.
Neither of us is perfect, but we can be perfectly imperfect together.
You don't have to be afraid, sad or lonely any more – I'm not leaving, now or ever.
I can't promise you the moon or stars, even that I'll never make mistakes ...
But I can promise you that you never have to face the storms alone anymore.
I can promise that I'll never stop loving you or giving our relationship my very best.
You're never too old to start believing in magic.

I know I'm not.

It won't be easy, it won't be fast, but with love in our hearts and courage in our souls, we can take this journey – you and I.

One step at a time.

I can't promise that we won't stumble or lose our way,

But if we face it all together,

I can promise it will always be worth it.

Maybe This Cage Has Been a Cocoon All Along

I never thought I'd find a way out of my mess, that I would stay buried in my problems.

Sometimes, it's easier to believe that the bad stuff is all you are meant to be.

I didn't think I had the courage or strength to fight for more, never believed I possessed the fire to rise from the ashes.

It's funny how life has a way of working itself out if you recognize the opportunity in front of you.

I stopped staring at the closed doors and started looking for the right open ones.

I had always listened to the lies whispering to my heart that I wasn't good enough ...

Not anymore.

As I wiped the tears from my eyes and the cleared the pain from my soul, I began to realize the truth I'd always missed.

Instead of dwelling in my misery, I needed to understand this wasn't a time to suffer ...

It was a time to prepare for my revival.

I stopped listening to dead-end ex partners and people who would keep me down, and I started listening to my heart.

I didn't just become stronger, aware and able, I woke those things buried deeply inside that just needed to be stirred ...

So I shook my foundations, sparked a fire in my spirit and clawed my way out of the darkest place I'd ever known.

It wasn't easy, it wasn't fast and it hurt deeply some days, but slowly I saw a light where before there'd only been darkness.

Truth is, I still have days that knock me down, moments when the breath gets stolen from me, and I still want to cry sometimes.

That's when I take a deep breath and force a smile through the tears that no longer shackle me.

I know now that the bad times were never the cage I once thought they were –

They were necessary for my journey to awaken my truth, to spark my rebirth and realize my strength.

I thought I was down and out and meant to stay in that darkness, but the reality is ...

That cage was never permanent,

It was a cocoon – incubating me, preparing me ...

For the greatest miracle of all:

Finally finding my wings and flying high ...

Like I was meant to do, all along.

This is a new day and a new chapter.

Reborn and revived,

This is my time –

Time to rise and shine, always.

To Laugh Forever with Someone You Take Seriously

Have I told you lately that you're just my kind of weird?
Before you, I always felt like I was the only one with my kind of sense of humor – a little different, sometimes twisted, always lively.
I've never been able to have an entire conversation with someone else through a single look ...
Until you.
All my jokes that no one else ever gets, you do in a way that just makes me smile.
The funny and unique glances across the room between us speak volumes.
We speak our own language – words and phrases that no one else in the world would ever understand ... And that's the beautiful thing about us:
They don't have to.
You just get me in ways I can't explain, and I wouldn't trade that for anything.
You can finish my sentences and understand a single look.
In fact, we can hold an entire conversation with just a solitary glance.
That's something that's very rare and wonderful.
Maybe it's strange that sometimes you know what I want even before I do.
But that's not something I want to ever change.
My true love showed up with mismatched socks, a crooked halo and warped sense of humor.

I wouldn't want it any other way.

That's the real magic of having your very own unique fairy tale.

It starts in your own style and ends with your own special happy ending.

I didn't see you coming, and I never could have imagined a love like ours ...

But I'll always smile when I remember how much I'm loved by you.

She Showed Him Another Way

If she knew one thing about him, it was that he was
not just a strong man,
But perhaps the strongest man she'd ever known.
She saw past the tough exterior and rugged façade
… she saw a beautiful and vulnerable soul that
longed for expression.
He'd been told all his life that men had to be hard,
be tough and that vulnerability was a weakness.
Looking at him lovingly, she took his hand and found
his eyes with hers.
Her voice, soft and soothing, was the one thing that
could melt his defenses.
"My dearest man, you are the strongest person I've
ever met but … there is another way."
His eyebrows furrowed as he looked at her,
perplexed and curious.
She smiled warmly.
"I see you … even the parts you hide from everyone
else. I know there's a side of you that longs to be
free. A gentler, more vulnerable part of your soul. In
fact, that's the part of you that's most beautiful of
all."
She could tell he knew her words rang true, but that
he'd never had the chance to fully embrace all of
himself.
He was known for his strength, his courage and his
ability to overcome anything.
But for all his ferocity, he'd never found someone to
love him for everything he was … and all that he
wanted to be.

Pressing her forehead softly to his, eyes fluttering, she kissed him gently and saw the battle raging in his eyes.

Her voice, barely a whisper, soothed his fiery debate.

"My love, the strongest of us aren't those who live and die by the sword, but those who are able to be the beautiful balance of strong and sensitive.

You don't have to sacrifice anything about who you are to become who you're meant to be … except to realize your happiness is more important than anyone else's perception."

Tears streamed down his face as she wiped them lovingly away with her warmest smile.

She had found a survivor and seen what none of the others ever glimpsed in his soul.

She loved him not just for who he was, but everything she knew he wanted to be.

Unconditionally without judgement, she was his safe place in a harsh world.

He could finally become the man he'd always tucked away, hiding and hopeful that one day, he could embrace who he truly was, instead of what he had always been told he should be.

On that fateful winter day, he discovered the love he'd waited his entire life to find in her.

In all his travels, for all that he had done and seen, she was the one thing he'd never experienced: true love.

There was nothing that would ever compare to what he found in her heart, in her arms.

Home.

The Keepers

They're the family you choose,
the friends who you're always close to,
no matter how often you talk.
If it's an hour, month or year, the conversation
between your hearts will never miss a day.
The people you call when you can't call anyone else.
They know you better, sometimes, than you know
yourself, and you wouldn't have it any other way.
They accept you unconditionally, cheer you through
the triumphs and face the battles by your side.
They're there for you when no one else is,
because they know your heart and hear your soul.
They're your people, the keepers of your deepest
truths ...
They guard your secrets, your dreams and your
fears.
The ones who stick around for a lifetime, who you
meet for a reason, not just a season.
They know you for who you really are and love you
without judgement,
Even when you're a complete mess and drive them
absolutely bonkers.
That's why they're special ... they just get you.
The people that pick up your pieces and
Celebrate your victories.
It doesn't matter how high you fly or how low you've
fallen, they're always there, waiting for you with a
hug.
You don't measure them by how far away they are,
but by how much you love them.

They're your friends, but they're so much more than that.

They're the people who are always there for you, the ones who have your back, no matter when or where.

Your ride or dies, your besties, your confidants, your people.

They're the family that you choose, each and every day ...

As you have since the first time you met them.

Those are the special ones.

Keep them close – together, you'll make memories that will last a lifetime.

Dreams are always better when shared with the people close to your heart.

They're the ones that you will always love –

Your friends ... the keepers.

I Miss You in Waves and Tonight I'm Drowning

I was never a person to miss someone.
I valued my independence and celebrated my
solitary life ...
Until you showed up and decided to turn my world
upside down.
Love doesn't even begin to describe the depth of us,
and missing you falls short of saying how much I
need you with me.
There aren't adequate words in any language that I
can find that will ever convey how I feel about you.
The moment when my lips part from yours and I
leave your side, wistful ...
Is the split second I feel incomplete.
You don't cross my mind ...
You never leave it.
Yet, we're never truly apart,
for I carry you with me, tucked away safely in my
heart.
No matter how hard my days may be or how life can
wear me down,
I know that I have something special waiting for me.
Your arms, your smile, your love.
For even at my weakest, you hear the song in my
heart and sing it back to me when I forget the words.
I could write a thousand love stories and countless
fairy tales, and yet nothing my pen could weave ...
Would ever compare to what you mean to me.
My best friend, my soulmate, my forever love.

You're my happy place ...
Thank you for being you.
It's changed my life, my heart, my future.
Right now ...
I just need your arms around me.
That's one of the feelings I love the most.
I love being in love with you.

Untying the Box of Lies

All my life, I was told who to be and what to do.
Everyone was always so concerned about making
sure I fit their labels ...
How to act, how to talk, how to look.
And truthfully, most of my life, I listened.
I did what I thought I was supposed to do until one
day, something changed in me.
I discovered that everything that "they" told me
wasn't for me at all ...
It was to make them feel and seem better.
It wasn't about my happiness, it was about their
control.
Once the box of untruths they fed me started to
unravel, I began to finally see the reality.
My truth.
Who I am, what I want and how I wanted to be.
No more would I chase their dreams and live by their
words, but instead, I would make my own way.
My life by my rules with my own style.
They told me I couldn't be different.
They laughed and mocked me for wanting more.
They didn't understand my authenticity, and that's
okay ...
They don't have to.
I don't need their spotlight, because I shine from
within ... in the way that I want to.
It's better to displease everyone for doing what you
know is right rather than please everyone else and
make yourself unhappy.
I'm done with all that.

I'm done dressing how I should, acting how I should and living everyone else's dream.

This is my time and my life, and I'm going to start chasing the dreams that do more than make me happy ...

I want the life and adventures that fill my soul, electrify my spirit and rouse my heart.

No more existing in their world and pretending to be happy.

In fact, no more pretending at all.

I may not always have the answers, and somedays, I forget where I'm going, but I'll always get there ... on my terms.

They tried to tame me and clip my wings so that I'd never uncover the truly colorful beauty of who I really am.

I have discovered the vibrant uniqueness of my soul, and I'm rising out of the depths they'd have kept me in.

You can't cage a beautiful spirit, and that's exactly who I am.

I finally understand that I'm wonderful, wild and now, I'm free.

For the first time in my life ...

I'm truly smiling, inside and out.

Why?

Because it's my time to shine.

Beautifully Broken

You don't need to be fixed, because you're not
broken in the way the world thinks.
You're cracked in just the right ways to let the light in
– from the pressure of a life well lived to a spirit that
won't ever give up.
You are a beautiful disaster,
a wonderful mess and
a perfect chaos, the kind of person whose courage
and strength defines the true nature of beauty.
You're the survivor who struggled, fought and
overcame everything, against all odds.
Because that's just who you are:
Lover, fighter, friend, dreamer.
You never stopped believing in yourself and in love,
though what you've been through would have
threatened to destroy a weaker person.
But not you.
Your wings weren't simply made to soar, but rather
to carry you to all the places that you've never even
seen –
Sometimes, chasing dreams requires flying high and
believing in yourself,
Perhaps even the path to love itself ...
Which can be downright frightening at times.
Find the one who loves you because of your
complex individuality and knows you are beautifully
scarred in the best ways possible.
No one is perfect and everyone has flaws.
Embrace your imperfections and appreciate your
uniqueness.

Your soulmate, best friend and lover will see,
understand and appreciate all that you are, all that
you've been and all that you're still yet to become.
That's real love – not that the fairy tale kind of magic,
but real, gritty and honest love,
Without judgment or prejudice,
With open arms and heart ...
One without end or apology.
It may not be perfect,
But it just might be perfect for you.
In the end, that's what matters most of all.
That, and your beautiful heart and wild spirit that will
always be free ...
Wild, free and worthy of true love.

I Need You to Be Real When Nothing Else Is

When the night closes in around you, and
You feel as though you don't know where to turn ...
Look to me.
When the world has gone mad and nothing seems
to make sense ...
Find my waiting embrace.
When the day knocks you down, and you can't seem
to find your way ...
Make your way to me.
When you're at your wit's end and the noise around
you deafens your thoughts ...
Turn to me.
There'll be days when you're at your worst and just
need to find some solace amidst the chaos ...
Those are the days that I'll be there, holding your
hand until we find the sunlight again.
My hand in yours, hearts in unison, together, we'll
dance in the darkest of rainstorms.
We won't always have the answers or know the way,
but walking side by side, we will figure it out ...
somehow, some way.
I can't promise you the moon or stars, the sun or
sky,
But I can always promise to be true and faithful to
you and our love.
You're my hope, my truth and my cherished angel,
And I'll always be your rock, your constant and the
safe place you call home.

So, when nothing else in this world seems to make
sense,
And everything around you is crashing down,
Look into my eyes and realize that I'll always be
there for you, I'll be real ...
When nothing else is.
'Til the horizons crash into the sea
and the night wind ceases to be,
I'll still be loving you.
Forever and a day.

Holding My Darkness, Shining My Light

I've fought my way through the hard days and the sadness, picked up the pieces of a broken heart more times than I can count.

I always asked why should I keep trying?

Life was never easy and love always failed me, so what was the point?

I had all the questions but didn't know any answers.

Behind my smile, the world never saw the tears I cried quietly to myself ...

In the shower, in the car ... wherever the sadness seized me.

I always snapped out of the angst and slapped on a happy face.

Truth was, I was dying inside and just needed a little bit of hope.

I thought I needed someone else to give me what I needed all along – love, hope, anything so that I could be fixed ...

Because surely I was broken inside, and no one else was like me, not to mention no one would love me, as messed up as I was.

Loneliness has a way of holding onto your heart until you find a light, a way out.

Sometimes, the beacon of hope isn't what you expect at all.

As the little boy in front of me in line at the store dropped his gum on the floor, I picked it up and gave it back to him, smiling.

He grinned sheepishly and giggled.

"You're pretty ... and I can see the pretty light

behind your eyes, too. Can you see it?"

Stunned, I found myself beaming and smiling back.

"Yes, little one, I think I might be able to ... now.
Thank you."

Nothing happens by chance, ever.

That was the day my life began to change.

I stopped asking "why me" and started asking "why
not me?"

I began to believe in myself, and for the first time, I
found the answers in the most unlikely place ...
Myself.

My heart had always known the way, I had just
forgotten how to get there.

I regained my lost strength, threw my sadness into
my past and dropped the baggage.

I'll never be perfect, and I'm good with that.

I'm real, authentic and I'm kind ... with a hint of
passion and ferocity mixed in.

I discovered a way to be brave through the dark
days and happy through the hard nights.

It wasn't easy and may never be, but I'll be okay ... I
found my answers within.

I know it's always darkest before dawn.

I discovered how to fall in love with being alive
and cherish all the small things I used to take for
granted.

I don't need to be saved, fixed or loved by someone
else to be happy.

And in the most unexpected way, in the most
unexpected place ...

In that little boy's smile ... I found the beginning of
the most perfect love of all:

The love of myself.
There is no one better to love me than me.
New chapter, new heart.
This is my happily ever after ...
My way.

There Are Many Men, But Few Gentlemen

No love story I've ever read started with "Your place or mine?"

In the fairy tales, the heroes don't disrespect the ladies.

Times are changed, and stories may be different, but the tenets remain the same:

Character. Honor. Respect. Chivalry. Passion.

Be a man of quality and let your manners speak for you.

Actions of dignity, not words of pretense.

If you seek a true lady's hand, begin with her heart.

Games are for boys.

Cheap sex is for shallow men.

True and respectful love is the way of the gentleman.

Capture her imagination, inspire her mind and stimulate her senses.

Class doesn't need a suit to impress a lady, but a gentleman knows both are essential.

Open her door, hold the umbrella, bring the car to the door.

Make her forget why her heart was ever broken before you.

Prove to her that all men aren't the same.

Chivalry isn't dead.

Show her you're the reason why.

Then, spend the rest of your days reminding her all over again.

Every day … falling in love.
One moment, one chance, one kiss..
That's all we truly seek in this journey called love.
Protect her heart, cherish her soul and inspire her spirit.
A boy by birth,
a man by age,
but a gentleman by choice.
Choose class instead of crass.
Anyone can act without honor and respect.
Take the high road while the rest play it safe.
If you want a lady, be a gentleman.
Ladies, if you want a gentleman, carry yourself with class.
My dear men, man up, stand up and step up.
She'll make you forever glad you did.
You'll make a believer out of her when you tell her, "I'll always be a gentleman."
Then do just that, for the rest of your days.

The Bravest Souls Follow Their Heart's Desire

I learned a long time ago to stop asking for permission and forgiveness for who I am and what I want.
I don't need a spotlight; I shine from within.
But there are some people who don't want anyone shining brighter than them.
That's okay, they can follow my stardust and soul shine as long as they want.
I'm not dampening my brilliance so that someone else can try to steal it away.
I'm authentic, I'm genuine and I'm real in every way, every day.
I'm not going to stand in your shadow, and I'm not seeking approval for being wonderfully awesome.
I don't even need you to understand my magic, because I'm unapologetically happy in my own skin.
Maybe you don't always get me, and truthfully, I don't either.
There are days that I wake up not knowing which way is up or why I want to cry for no reason.
But you can count on me to show up, stand up and always be shining.
Sometimes, there may be tears behind my eyes and clouds over my soul, but I own that about myself. I made peace with my beautiful angst a long time ago.
I realize I may not make sense sometimes, but that's all just part of my indescribable soulfulness.
I live and love by my heart, and I don't always take

my head with me.

I love hard when there's love to be had, and I chase my dreams with relentless optimism and unbridled passion.

When you look at me, you're never going to wonder where I stand or what I'm thinking, because you'll be the first to know.

I know I'm not always the easiest to love, but that's the part of my spirit that makes me so amazing.

I'll always be a beautiful disaster and gorgeous mess who keeps life interesting.

What's the point of just going through life merely existing?

I want to live … truly live – frenetically alive with the feelings that no one can ever take away from me …

To know that I've tasted the best of life, chased the wildest dreams and experienced the most vibrant essences of the world,

That is what I want.

Forget ordinary days and lukewarm coffee, I want to be immeasurably alive every single day.

So, if you want to take my hand and embrace the impossible, I welcome your company.

I'll never let fear of failure define me.

No matter where I go and what I do, I'll always chase it with my distinctive flair.

I'm not for the faint of heart, and I wouldn't have it any other way.

So, if you think you can handle my magic and embrace life by my side, then let's go find some adventure.

My dreams will never have an expiration, and my

magic is boundless.
The question is ...
Can you handle my raw and authentic truth?
Together,
Let's go fall in love with being alive ...
every day.

Being Her Own Everything

She grew through adversity,
finding her strength when being strong became her
only option.
She realized that real strength isn't about how long
you can hold out before breaking ...
It's about how much you can overcome after you
have already broken.
When she stopped defining her happiness through
the eyes of others,
When she discovered that being someone's
"something" just wasn't enough anymore,
That's when she began to truly awaken.
She ceased being a spark and started becoming a
fire.
She realized that burning with passionate intensity
and self-satisfaction completed her in a way that
another person never could.
She had to love herself before she could truly love
another.
Meaningful silence meant more to her than
meaningless words,
And she learned to listen to her soul and follow her
heart.
She made mistakes, stumbled and fell, but knew
that growth takes time.
Even the brightest diamonds are formed under
intense pressure, and not quickly.
That's when she realized how brightly she could
shine within herself.
She found a strength that she never knew she

possessed in places she had never before known to look.

Life, love and respect were no longer about being perfect and accepted.

She was imperfectly beautiful in all the ways she loved,

Wonderfully flawed and uniquely chaotic,

She learned to thrive on her mistakes and evolve from her failures.

Becoming her own "everything" empowered her to continually improve and become more.

She didn't need anyone or anything to realize her dreams and find her happiness,

Her heart and soul were wild and free.

She found herself, and more than that,

She discovered her authentic and visceral truth.

No one could ever take that away from her, her hopes, her fears, her heart:

It made her who she was, and she wouldn't change a thing.

She had no more interest in the flawless people anymore.

The ones that burned her bridges only illuminated her way to a better place.

She surrounded herself with the souls that understood and accepted her for all of her flawed beauty and disastrous ways.

Give her the cracked souls that meshed perfectly with her broken pieces.

Her dream never came with an expiration.

She smiled because she knew ...

All her broken roads led her exactly where she was

always meant to be.
She'd found her way home ...
And came to love herself in the process.

Now and For Always

Promise me this, for now and always:
Promise me your heart, to have and hold, 'til life takes my last breath.
Promise me your love, until the whisper of time slips away.
Promise me your passion, so we may always know the fire that unites our hearts.
Promise me your soul, so that I may uncover all that you are 'til the end of our days.
Promise me kisses to welcome me home,
Hugs to remind me I'm safe and
Your touch to assure me it'll all be okay.
Promise me to share all the big moments as well as all the little ones in between.
Promise me to always stand beside me, facing every storm and challenge, hand in hand.
Promise me your respect, and I'll do the same.
Promise me your first thought daily and your last as you drift off to sleep …
And may a smile find you as you think of me.
Those are but a few of the promises I'll cherish from you,
As well as the promises I will make:
I promise to love you without question,
be loyal without end and be yours without fail.
I promise to love you, now and always, for who you are and who you will always be.
I promise to always be your best friend, your soulmate and forever love …
unconditionally, until we find each other in the next

life.
I promise now and for always ...
To love you, endlessly.

No One Saw the Pain Behind Her Eyes

She was strong because that was her only option.
She didn't know how to be anything else; she was a survivor.
Her heart was hidden behind walls because that's how she endured the pain …
She faced the world behind a happy façade.
She tucked away the tears behind her smile, hid the pain underneath her laughter.
Her soulful eyes spoke a very different story, if you took the time to get past her deeply woven countenance of enigmatic mystery.
Most never did, and she was fine with that.
She loved her way and on her terms.
She was a strong woman who had fought brokenness, failures and broken hearts.
A girl with dreams who grew into a survivor with scars.
Her wounds didn't define her or defeat her, they forged her wisdom.
Her broken road built her strength.
Her cracks from hard days eventually became the ways the light illuminated her soul.
The fire would never claim her.
Instead, she became a fiery phoenix.
There were those times, though,
When the sadness overwhelmed her and the tears became part of her story.
The silence at night could deafen her with the onslaught of emotions.
She may not have been the bravest nor the most

beautiful,
But she was determined to become the most unforgettable.
She used her fear as fuel,
And her pain as motivation,
To never be broken again, but instead to let her light shine through the healed fissures of her heart.
She was a volatile tempest of emotions,
A magnificent mess and beautiful disaster,
And she was always true to herself.
Everyone would say she was the happiest of women,
But that was because they didn't know her sorrows.
No one would want that burden … or so she thought.
She soon realized that the truest of loves, whether friends or soulmates, would always embrace her heaviest baggage ...
And help her unpack.
She discovered that joy works better in twos,
But she didn't know if she could trust another man after the countless disappointments.
Her heart had been crushed so many times, and her hopes had crumbled away.
She had once stopped finding reasons to believe in true love again ...
Until some long-forgotten stardust somehow sprinkled itself onto her soul.
The reason, against all odds, found her.
She had sometimes wondered if she was even worthy of love.
But what she realized was that she was worthy of

the greatest love, and it all started with her.
When she finally learned to truly love herself she also began to open her heart.
She knew the sun would always rise and maybe, just maybe, there was hope for a brighter tomorrow.
She knew that somewhere beyond all the storms,
There was a rainbow waiting just for her.
It was always darkest before dawn ...
And it was time for the rise of her new day ... her new chapter.
One blustery day, as it fate would have it, around a random corner, a curious thing happened on the way to forever.
Real and lasting love smiled on her ...
And she never looked back.
She didn't know where tomorrow might lead, all she knew was that
Finally, for the first time in as long as she could remember ...
she had hope.

A Fairy Tale Kind of Love … with a Few Passionate Chapters Mixed In

She was much like anyone else,
Except for a few small differences that most never even realized or knew.
She had truths that didn't define her, they empowered her.
To the world, she embodied class.
She lived with a free conscience and fierce spirit.
She always took pride in being a lady,
Manners, courtesy and dignity were her calling cards.
Educated, intelligent and eloquent,
She was never without something to say and always had a voice that was heard.
What most never discovered …
Was that her most articulate and colorful side was completely hidden and walled off …
past the high heels and skirts,
Behind the walls and pretty façade,
Underneath the captivating smile she wore proudly.
She didn't need to share her deeper desires with the world, those weren't for just anyone.
She reserved that for her special someone –
The one person who was able to see her for who she truly was and understand that part of her.
If everyone only knew, they'd be surprised that the delicate lady burned with white hot intensity.
Truthfully, the thought made her giggle a bit, how the uptight and conforming masses squirmed with the

fires of desire.

She knew who she was and what she wanted.

Ordinary passion didn't interest her; in fact, it bored her immensely.

Wild, passionate desire permeated her darkest, deepest places.

She needed more than lackluster passion and paltry physical need.

She wanted it all – fire, love, passion and desire ... but more than just of the flesh.

Lesser men had tried – and failed – to claim her on their terms.

They never really saw her for the amazing woman she was, and she didn't waste her energy on superficiality.

If you couldn't enchant her – mind, body and soul – then she wasn't interested ...

She knew what she wanted, and she hungered for the one who could find his way past her defenses, enchant her mind and melt her heart.

She wasn't afraid to push her boundaries,

Craving the things that immersed her into desire without restraint.

She didn't do it to be different or for the sake of pleasing anyone else,

She did it simply because that's what she wanted.

She yearned to be completed and fulfilled for the amazing woman she was ...

Sensual, strong, proud and feisty.

That's what made her whole, that's what made her happy.

She made no apologies for who she was or what

she enjoyed.
She had her own kind of fairy tale.
She was an angel with a crooked halo,
With the most passionate thoughts,
Hidden behind a ladylike exterior.
She couldn't be tamed and dared any to try.
They soon learned the truth of her:
When she was wild, she was free.

The One Who Completes You

And then, all of the love songs were about you ...
Now, I almost can't remember life before you and
how I was ever happy any other way but in your
arms.
Some things are just meant to be – you made me
understand that from the moment we met ...
Now I can't and won't see my life and my future any
other way.
I fell in love with you, and now I know why this is the
greatest feeling I've ever experienced.
There's no place that I'd rather be than in your heart.

A Woman Has the Right to Be Two Things: Who and What She Wants

For all the people who tell you that you can't ...
All the ones who'd have you believe that you'll never make it ...
Give them a crash course in who you are and what you can do.
You're a person with goals and dreams,
not something to be objectified.
If they can't give you a fair chance based on your abilities, not your looks, then move on.
Don't let them tell you what you can and can't do.
Never accept anyone else's definition of who you are.
This is your life and your shot.
No one can take that away from you unless you let them.
Let them stare at you while you walk away – they'll miss the best thing that's ever happened to them as you saunter right out of their lives.
It's their loss, cause you're moving up while they're standing still.
Just because they are stuck in the dark ages doesn't mean you have to be stuck with them.
While you're focused on the light at the top,
they are concerned with all the wrong things.
When they finally realize that you've moved on and achieved great things, you'll be long gone on the road to success.
The weak man will say she has an attitude.

The strong man will love her spirit.
If they don't want you on your terms,
then you don't need them on theirs.
Let them think what they want.
Success doesn't recognize gender.
If you've got dreams to catch, chase them however you want –
High heels, sneakers or barefoot.
Just make sure you do it on your terms, with your style, in your own way.
They're your dreams.
Don't ever let anyone tell you differently.
Smile …
It's your time to shine, baby.

The Greatest Gift

He walked away, stealing away so many of my hopes and dreams in an instant.
Truthfully, it was my fault for giving him that power, but I'd always been the one to follow my heart and fell in love hard when I did.
As he left, I realized that losing myself in what was once "us" had destroyed everything I thought I had been.
The days and nights seemed to run together as my heart bled the pain of broken dreams and lost love.
I'd lost myself in what he wanted me to be and, in the end, he had cast me aside without care.
I didn't hear his words as he tore apart my heart, only the bleeding emotions that were sinking my soul.
When the one thing you believe will always be forever vanishes into yesterday, it shakes your foundations to the very core.
Somewhere along your spiral to the depths of discontent,
You lose everything that you once believed to be true about yourself.
You stop believing the good things and begin to hear only the negativity that slowly seeps into your soul.
The bad is always easier to believe than the good … especially when you've lost yourself and your heart has shattered into countless pieces.
But that's the thing about being broken – the light slowly begins to permeate the cracks of your broken soul … if only you let it.

Piece by piece, I forged the fires that once consumed me into lighting my new path.

I didn't always know where I was going or even how to was going to get there, but as time passed, I became more determined on my journey back to a better me ... a happier place.

Losing yourself means that you have the chance to rise from the ashes, stronger than ever before ... to create a stronger self.

I took the small acts of self love along the way and began to finally understand who I was meant to be all along.

In the end,

He gave me the greatest gift possible by turning his back on me ...

His choice led me to the path that breathed life into a brighter and better future ahead.

I turned my wounds into wisdom and my setback into a comeback.

I no longer accepted less than I deserved, and I finally realized my worth.

I was worthy of the best –

From myself and every one in my life ...

I learned the most important truth of all:

Strong people aren't born, they're forged by the fires they walk through.

I turned my can'ts into cans and my dreams into plans.

Rise or shine, I'll always give what I get, and I have a lot of love to share.

I'll never let my past define me, and I'll always let my passion breathe life into my dreams.

Most of all, I realized the most wonderful gift of all:
I don't have to be perfect ...
Because I won't ever be anything close to that ...
I just have to be me.
My story will always be a tale with failures, crashes and loss ...
But more than that,
It'll be about rising again and shining brightly.
I'm strong, I'm worth it,
And I'll always be more than enough.

Her Anchor, His Wings

He's something she's never known –
A safe place for her heart, a harbor midst any storm
that she might face.
He's her rock, her strength, her reason.

She's unlike anyone he's ever met,
She sparkles when she talks,
She shines when she smiles,
Her light infuses brightly into his very soul.

He does more than dance with her demons,
He soothes her deepest fears with his touch.
Her moods and battles just seem to balance out
When he places his hand in hers.

He didn't know what it meant to not be alone,
Used to standing strong and living solo,
He wasn't used to someone who would be there,
Supporting him like she does through it all.

He lives in a way that makes her pulse race,
Invigorating her spirit with his fearless attitude,
He brings her to edge of the wild before
Whispering to her soul of love's promise.

She brings a peace to his heart he's never found,
A place of rest that whispers to him in the quiet,
Telling him it's okay to be himself, to be loved,
That he's safe with her, in her arms, forever.

No matter her flights of fancy,
Regardless where her mind may wander,
When she's settled back to earth,
She knows the solace she found in him, her anchor.

He never knew how to chase his dreams,
Let his hopes and spirit soar with the heavens
Until she showed up and made him realize,
Sometimes you have to find the wings you had all
along.

They were a pair unlike any other,
Checks and balances, yin and yang.
They completed each other like a jigsaw puzzle,
Found each other against impossible odds,
Believing when love seemed so far away,
They discovered the most unlikely thing in an
improbable way.

The perfectly imperfect love of two people
Who never gave up on the dream that
One day, they too,
Would find their happily ever after.
They found that and so much more ...
In each other, now and for always.

The Light from My Soul

Once, if you'd asked me about love,
I'd have told you that it wasn't real and happily ever after didn't exist –
Just made up stories to read about and give people hope.
Truth is, I was tired of having my heart broken and my hopes dashed with another dead-end relationship.
Forevers always turned into nevers, and hellos faded away into goodbyes.
Every time love slips through your fingers,
you lose a little bit more of yourself ... and hope.
I started wondering what was wrong with me, why I wasn't good enough.
Those are the times when I cried for no reason and stayed in bed all day because I just couldn't face the world.
Everyone told me that I'd be okay, but deep down, I wondered if that could ever be true.
I read all the words and searched for a spark among the downpour of pain.
Worse than that, though, is the emptiness.
Try as I might to fill the void in my heart, nothing ever helped heal my bleeding soul ...
Emotions poured out as I just wanted to be okay ... and didn't know if I could be, not in any way that mattered.
The thing about the silence, it can be truly deafening when you're all alone with the thoughts in your mind.
Somewhere along the way, I just chose to wake up.

Dwelling in my misery wasn't making me feel any better, so why stay where I'm not happy?
I didn't.
I chose to find a way out into the light, because anywhere was better than staying down and out.
It wasn't easy, and honestly, there are still days when I need a few minutes to close my eyes and breathe.
The storms still come and the nights can still be long, but I've come to realize that I'm not alone if I truly open myself up to my people – the ones I love and care about.
I know now that no matter the pain I've felt and the wounds I've suffered, I can rise again from the ashes ...
Stronger, scarred and wiser for where I've been.
My heart's been battered and bruised, but it's still beating strong ...
In fact, it's more vibrantly alive than ever ...
That's what happens when you believe in yourself and the power of your dreams.
Sometimes, you have to lose yourself along the way to discover the path to where you were meant to be.
The ones that cast me aside weren't ever my people ... they were my lessons, my reasons to find the light in my once blackened darkness.
I won't say that I don't lose my way some days, because I do.
I can't say that my life is exactly where I want it to be, but it's getting there.
I'm nowhere close to perfect, and I'll never be, but maybe that's my power ...

Being beautifully disastrous and wonderfully imperfect
Makes me real, authentic and original.
I'll never take back where I've been and the pain I've felt, because that's just what I needed to find my soul shine.
I'll never change the love I've given or the hope I've felt, because I'll always believe in the power of my dreams.
Most of all, I'll never let the cracks from a broken past keep the light from illuminating my soul ...
And that is why I will always be ...
Real, passionate and shining from within.
I'm going sparkle that love everywhere.

The Love of a Guarded Woman

When she says she loves you, it's not because she needs you.
It's just the opposite.
It's because she wants and chooses you, every day, in every way.
She's a strong woman who doesn't need anyone, to be honest.
So, if she opens her heart and soul to you, don't hesitate or take the opportunity for granted ...
You may only get the briefest of chances to win her over – heart, mind and soul.
But be careful with the chance to love her as you've been given ...
Understand that she's been hurt, bruised and scarred, and that's part of her beauty.
She's guarded because her heart has been broken, and she loves fiercely.
She won't accept anything less than your best and she'll never settle.
She doesn't protect herself out of callous insensitivity, but rather out of self-preservation.
She's been down this road before, and she wants to be loved and give love freely ... not to repeat the pain of past broken hearts.
Her love is earned carefully and cautiously – and because she is worth the price.
Any price.
She knows her value and won't sacrifice her standards or sell herself short.
Loyal, passionate and true, she doesn't want just

anyone … she wants the one.
Forget the one night guys, she wants a gentleman who desires all of her nights.
She's not a one in a million girl.
She's a once in a lifetime woman.
Stick around and you'll see exactly why
She's worth it all.
Put aside your pride, explore her most vulnerable depths and engage her soul …
Utterly, honestly and completely.
She's giving you a chance to uncover the truth of all that she is, because she chooses you.
Love her tenderly, respectfully and most of all, devotedly.
She'll show you why happily ever after isn't just a phrase.
It's her truth.
She is and always will be playing for keeps.
Beautiful,
Strong and free.

Even Cinderella Just Wanted a Night Off and a Great Pair of Heels

I don't need to be fixed, saved or changed.
I'm happy just the way I am, and I'm rocking a great attitude, a happy outlook and a never say never mindset.
I'm not holding out for a hero, I decided to become my own.
If you think I'm just a challenge for a notch on your belt, look elsewhere.
I'm not a trophy, an option or a challenge.
If you need one of those, go find a race to run.
I'm a strong person, a deep soul and a wildfire love.
I'm not for the faint of heart, and I'll never accept second best in anything or anyone.
If you can't give me the respect, courtesy and appreciation I deserve, then I'll find someone who will.
Some will say I have an attitude problem, I'd say that they don't like strong people.
I give what I get, and I don't put anything less than my all into my friendships, my life and my love.
Save the shallow values for other people, I need soulful people with deep feelings and fiery hearts.
I'm not perfect, in fact, far from it.
There's days when I cry into my coffee for no reason and take an hour to figure out which shoes to wear.
That's just part of my infuriatingly fun personality …
or at least, that's what I'm going with.
I'll never have boring days or times without fun,

because life is made for living ...
Merely existing is for everyone else.
I don't just chase my dreams, I dive headfirst into following my heart.
Truth is, sometimes I forget to take my head with me, but I'm good with that.
No matter where life and love takes me, I'll do it my way with my own unique style ...
And no one can ever take that away from me.
I'm flawed and I'm imperfect, but I'm ridiculously awesome in all the ways that matter:
I love with intense devotion;
I live with reckless abandon;
and I tackle every day with zealous passion.
I'm going to fail, I'm going to fall and I'm going to make a mess out of myself sometimes ...
But that's what makes me beautiful.
I'm real, I'm authentic and I'm always original.
I may not always say what you want to hear, but I'll always give it to you straight.
So, if you want to love me the way I deserve and be a part of my life,
Then plan on meeting me halfway –
Equal, respected and loved.
I won't ever stop my life to chase love, but I'll always make time for the people that matter.
Now, it's up to you if you want to be one of my people.
I can't promise it will always be easy, or that I'll always be rainbows and sunshine ...
But in the end,
I can always promise that I'll be worth it.

Forget About Yesterday and Dream About Tomorrow

Love turns dead ends into possibilities and wrong turns into hope.
Then, just like that, nothing will ever be the same – but then, would you want it to be?
You stop wondering why not and start realizing why.
You're beautiful … and you'll find someone who shares that belief – inside and out.
You'll meet the one person whose jagged edges fit perfectly into your uneven corners and, the next thing you know,
you won't even remember what life was like before them.
And that's when you realize the truth of it all:
Love is unpredictable and arrives when the time is right – not a moment before.
You may get frustrated and a bit lonely as it seems as though love won't ever find you ...
But work on being the best version of yourself and let fate unfold as it's meant to ...
With an open heart and mind.
I can't promise you it will be fast or that it will be easy, but it will always be worth it.
Two become one as love finds you ...
Eyes meet as hearts beat in unison, passion collides and souls unite.
Those who are meant to be in your heart will always find a way to your arms.
And when they do, cherish every moment of your

time together and drink in the love that fills your spirit.

That, my friends, is the intoxicating allure of forever that we all search for – and find – when the time is right.

Don't ever give up – you never know who or what is just around the corner.

I Know Who I Am, and I Own It

This is my life and my choice.
I know that I'm not everyone's cup of tea,
But I promise you I can definitely be your shot of expresso.
I'm spicy, I'm flashy and sometimes I'm sassy,
But you'll always know where you stand with me.
There's no maybe, possibly or hopefully in my life and my world.
What you see is what you get ... no more, no less.
I give what I get and ask only the same in return ...
Character.
Loyalty.
Passion.
Love.
Respect.
You don't have to love me or even like me,
But you will respect me.
I'll never let my friends down, put my dreams aside or sacrifice my values ...
And I love fiercely with all my heart.
I'm not always right, and I'm okay with that,
But the best part of life is figuring things out ... and getting it wrong, together.
Yes, I'll always have something to say,
but I won't waste my time or breath making small talk to people who don't care.
There are too many things in life that are worth discussing,
And I choose to be a voice, not an echo.
Don't confuse my occasional nonchalance with a

lack of passion, because I will always care about the people who matter.

Me, you and my circle.

I focus my time and energy on the best parts of my life ...

And just because I don't seem emotional doesn't mean I don't care ...

It just means I've mastered my poker face.

I'll always be original, real and authentic ...

I'll always speak my mind and share my truths – you'll know how I feel without a doubt.

I don't love halfway, and I don't live with regret.

I'll always do more than show up,

I'll rock it with high expectations and higher standards.

Some treat life like it's a game ...

Not me.

I don't have time to follow the crowds and be something I'm not.

I make my own rules.

This is my world, my way.

Win, lose or draw, it'll always be one amazing ride.

We're Not Perfect, but We're Perfect for Each Other

And all I ever wanted, I found wonderfully in you.
A perfect love between two imperfect people –
finding each other against impossible odds across
worlds apart.
Two souls, one heartbeat in a meeting 'twixt the
stars above … always meant to be and forever
joined in a love without end.
Perfectly imperfect together – and I'd have it no
other way.
That's the best happily ever after I could ask for …
Meant to be, real and forever.

I've Been Shattered, but I'm Still Standing

If you could see into the places past my eyes, you'd begin to understand a bit of who I am.
You'd know that behind my eyes are tears sometimes, not because I'm sad,
But because I'm still healing.
My soulful smile has many levels of happiness, I'm never going to be simply black or white.
To try to understand me is to dive into the depths of everything I am,
It's going to be a portrait of beautiful disaster and a rocky road … but it will be genuinely me.
You'll feel the pain radiating from my darkest depths and know that's how I survived –
That's the strength that pushed me to thrive.
I wasn't always brave and resilient, and the storms of my life tried to break me into a million pieces.
I turned to everyone and everything for answers yet only uncovered more questions.
You never really know how strong you are until being strong is the only option you have.
I never wanted to make the wrong choices and end up in the worst places.
I loved the people never meant for me and lost myself along the way.
I traded heartache for heartbreak time and again, and that became my version of love.
But, truth be told, somewhere in the darkness you choose to stay lost or you climb your way back in the

light.

Many times, I thought it was better to be lost than found in the misery that seemed to surround my life.
I didn't have the answers, but I figured out the right questions to ask, and one day,
I decided that I was done being a victim.
I chose to rise above, rise again and rediscover my wings.
It's kinda ironic how you can lose yourself on the broken road and somehow find the answers at the same time.
I'm not perfect nor do I always have it together, but I'm real, I'm authentic and I love every one of my jagged edges.
I'm not asking for acceptance or permission.
I have all the love I need right here in my heart.
I learned to love me for me.
I didn't fight my way back to the top to be judged harshly by fake people who neither care nor matter.
So, if you want to walk in my light, bring your own sparkle and sunshine with you.
My stardust, moonlight and magic may be the almost perfect recipe for an amazing future, if you take the time to really try to get me.
Once you realize my untamed fire isn't meant to be caged, then you'll be welcome to run wildly by my side.
So, if you've got passion in your heart, depth in your soul and wind in your spirit, then let's dance until the moon melts away into nothingness.
The night is young, and in this moment we can live forever.

I yearn for the one who can love me for me and even who I've yet to become ...

I've got a lot of love to give and a lot of feelings to share –

The question is ...

Do you have the heart and patience to understand and love me for each and every beautiful flaw that defines me?

Forgetting What You Feel, Remembering What You Deserve

I used to lose myself in the ones I thought would always be there,
The people that I had hoped would be loyal and never forsake my love.
I'm the kind of person who follows my heart and loves with every sliver of my soul ... it's just how I'm wired.
My friends always told me that I'd get hurt and my choices were not the best for me,
But I still dove headfirst into love.
Somewhere along the way, I started losing who I was as I tried to be what they wanted me to become.
Deep down, I knew that I wasn't really happy living that way, but their joy outweighed my truths.
Time and again, heartache turned into heartbreak and happily ever after fell apart with every failed relationship.
I thought it was me, that there was something wrong with me ...
Something that I was failing at, not doing or, worst of all,
That I didn't deserve to be happy.
Every broken road and shattered heart added one more wall to my hurting soul.
I became more and more guarded as the once hopeful dreams of forever melted away into another faded memory of love gone astray.
Somewhere along the way, my broken spirit and

wounded soul reached its lowest point and I lost all
faith in love ... and more importantly,
Myself.
I didn't believe I was good enough to be loved.
I saw myself through the failed vision of people who
never saw me for who I was.
That's when I realized that the truth was different
than I had come to believe all along.
I had always deserved more.
It was never my fault: they didn't really deserve me
or even understand who I was.
I stopped asking what was wrong with me and
started realizing what was wrong with them.
I know now that I couldn't make them love me in the
way that I deserved.
Respectful, deep and passionate love wasn't ever
going to be their way ...
But that's what I discovered I needed.
I craved the beauty of a real and genuine
relationship that fulfilled me with deeper purpose.
I stopped letting lesser people win my heart and
started remembering who I was and what I deserved
... On my terms, in the way that I chose ...
respectfully and passionately, without end.
I don't need to be chased, wooed or won.
I love myself now, so I don't need just anyone else
like I used to think I did.
I deserve and require,
More than anything,
Love on equal terms and with soulful depth,
I just want to be loved for me,
And I'm worth the wait.

You Never Think the Last Time is the Last Time

Tomorrow isn't promised to any of us, so seize the opportunity and live in the moment.
Make the most of the time you've been given – don't let chances to enjoy life and love slip away.
Appreciate those times when your heart is full ...
Capture those frozen instants of beautiful feelings and tuck them away in your heart, in your memories.
Don't miss an opportunity to express how you feel or let them know how special they are.
Tell her that you love her ... every chance you get.
Show him that you care about him, each and every day.
Celebrate more than the milestones and major events –
Do the little things and enjoy them.
Cook him dinner.
Run her bath and have a glass of wine waiting.
Plan a weekend getaway.
Hold hands during the movie.
Love a little longer, a little harder.
Leave her a love note.
Make him breakfast in bed.
Call in sick to stay home together and snuggle.
Book a hotel room in town for tonight.
Go on a picnic.
Have a date where you had your first date.
Take the time, make the chances and seize today.
Show them you love them in countless endless ways

... Don't let tomorrow come and leave you wishing you'd done more, said more, felt more.
Love with all your heart today ...
Passionately, patiently, unselfishly and deeply ...
Live fully in those moments and experience everything you can.
You deserve it, and you'll always remember these small treasure troves of time that warm your hearts.
Fall in love with each other and being alive ... all over again, every day.
Cherish it.
Enjoy it.
Savor it.
Make the moments into memories and you'll never say "what if."
That's the secret to a life well lived.
Love like this is your last chance and live like everything is a miracle.
Today, tomorrow and forever ...
Looking back, you'll be glad you did.

A Love That's Passionate in Private and Proud in Public

If you can't love me at my worst, then don't expect
my heart at my best.
Save the mediocre passion and mild love, I don't
believe in lackluster emotions.
I want to be loved like a wildfire and set my feelings
on fire with white hot intensity.
If you're not proud of our love to the world, then
don't expect me to long for your affection in private.
I'm not a secret or a person who will be hidden
away.
Love me loudly or don't love me at all.
I'll never be okay being an option when I should be
the priority.
I deserve to have a partner that will show the world
just how much I mean to them.
I want a wild and vibrant love affair, and I won't
accept anything less.
Real, raw and unapologetic passion is just who I am
and what I expect.
I'd rather have a wild ride than simply exist and
survive my days.
Give me the adventures that fill my soul, the times
that give me purpose and the love that sets my heart
on fire.
I'm not a maybe kind of person,
Don't expect me to be lukewarm or not have an
opinion ...
I'm always going to be "all in."

For the person I love, the people in my heart and the things I want.

I chase my dreams with reckless abandon, love with fiery passion and live without regret.

There are going to be days that I get it all wrong, but that's just part of my awesomeness –

I'm perfectly flawed and disastrously amazing,

And I'll always do it in my own unique way.

I don't ask for more than I'm willing to give, and I always give my all.

So, if you want to embrace this life by my side and passionately pursue love and happiness,

Then take my hand and let's see where the day takes us.

I don't wait for life to happen to me and I never will ...

I'll never look back and ask myself why I didn't listen to my heart.

So, the choice is yours –

Either step up and join me or step aside and let me go ...

Love me or leave me,

I'll always do it all with spirited passion and soulful purpose.

If I can't put my heart into it ...

I take myself out if it.

Come what may,

I'll always do it my way.

The Sound of My Name on Your Lips

At the end of the day when the world is deafening,
When life tries to bring me down,
I yearn to hear the solitary sound that
Makes me feel safe like nothing else can,
The one thing I'll never get enough of ...

The wonderful sound of my name upon your lips ...
The feelings it evokes,
The emotions that I feel,
And the love you've given to me for always.

When my phone rings and I see your name,
My heart races and my breaths become choppy,
For I know the beauty that comes next,
The one thing that serenades my soul endlessly ...
Your voice soothing my fervent heart.

When I first open my eyes, sun shining,
I need only look over at you beside me,
And my heart smiles in countless ways,
I'll hear the one thing I need so much every day ...
Your voice that comforts me when nothing else can.

As I take your face into my hands,
Our souls colliding as our lips melt together,
The sound that is unlike anything else
I've ever heard before calms my spirit.

The one thing that does all those things
Is but one and the same:

The sound of my name on your lips,
And how that beautiful whisper of love
Says so much in a single word.

Love forever, loyalty uncompromising,
Passion, desire and happily ever after.
That's just a smattering of the emotions
That the sound stirs in me,
And for that, I've fallen madly in love
with you ...

For always and forever will I cherish you,
until I find you in the next life once more.
Mate of my soul and lover of my heart,

You've given me much more than you'll
Ever know ...
You, me and forever ...
Beautiful in our eyes.

I Know How It Feels … But Hope is Forever

I sit alone in the dark wondering why it hurts so much.
I cry silent tears so that no one will realize my pain, the despair is almost physical.
I don't want anyone to know how much I suffer, because I don't seek help or want pity – there is no one who can lead me out of this funk.
My tear-stained cheeks are illuminated in the darkness, a glowing monument to my painful descent into angst.
The anguish, it overwhelms my senses, permeates my very soul as it slowly begins to feel real, and sears my skin with a slight burning sensation.
The clash of emotional embattlement resonates throughout my body, sending shockwaves across my skin.
Another night has fallen and so has my chance for quickly climbing my way out of the hopelessness.
The light seems so distant now, and I almost wonder how I will ever find it again.
The struggle has made me weary, and the doubt has filled my soul.
This battle is mine and mine alone – no one would understand my silent battle against something they don't understand …
Something I don't even get it sometimes.
Solace is gone and anguish washes across my spirit … and I cry.

I know how you feel in those darkest of nights, for I am there too, beside you, wondering how we keep going.

Nothing is ever easy – hope seems to vanish as quickly as the daylight.

But, I know that pain is temporary and hope is forever – it all depends on which cup I choose to drink from.

Yes, I'm down.

Yes, I feel like throwing in the towel.

But, it's always darkest before dawn, and the light shines the brightest in the blackest night.

It can't rain forever ...

I know I'm going to figure this out –

I won't rest until I see the path again.

It won't be easy and it won't be fast, but I know I'm better than this ...

I have moments of weakness, but I'm not weak.

I'm afraid, but then, everyone is sometimes.

I'm battered and broken, but that's how the light gets in.

Courage isn't the absence of fear, but having the strength to act in spite of it ...

To know what's most important ...

And then finding a way.

More than that, I know I'm more than this.

I can become anything I want and choose, but I know that the choice and the belief will always start with me.

Forged from fire,

The Phoenix will always rise again.

All I can tell you is that darkness doesn't last forever.

Everyone has different walks and while we're all damaged and broken, that's what makes us each beautifully unique ...
And what I remind myself of, every day.
We are never too broken to be worthy, to deserve love – especially self love ...
The most important love of all.
Sometimes, I learned, you just have to believe;
In love, in hope, in faith, or yourself – something, anything.
Find your something ... and just hold onto it.
It's that something, your reason, that will get you through the hard times.
As I open my eyes and wipe away the tears, I can't help but smile, even when I think I shouldn't have a reason to.

An envelope with your all too familiar writing catches my eye ...
Words to make me smile ... and to spark the slightest glimmer of hope.
Just like that, I realize that you have to see the signs when they arrive, no matter how small or seemingly unimportant.
A sign of hope, of love, of belief.
Open your mind and free your heart.
That's all you can do, sometimes, to make the pain go away –
If only for a few precious moments ...
And soon, those moments will catch on fire and your soul will start to come alive.
Love, like hope, burns eternal.

You and I, we're never alone.
Each and every day, I find a reason – any reason –
to believe, to hope ... to smile.
That is our way back to the light.
We can climb out of the darkness, one moment, one
smile, one day at a time.
If you stumble, know that I'll be there to grab your
hand and help you up.
Together, we can overcome anything.

*For all those who struggle, know that you are not
alone. Take my hand ... le t's walk together.
You're always welcome by my side.*

So Many Things I Wish for You

My wish for you, on this day and all others, is so
many things.
Sunrises to breathe life into your days,
Sunsets to warm your heart,
And rainbows to chase away the storms.
Laughter to bless your soul and beauty to enrich
your life.
May your moments be amazing and your days be
fulfilling.
May you always see the small things in life that
make you smile.
Kind words from a passerby, gentle thoughts from a
loved one.
Kindness from someone you meet, and comfort on
difficult days.
May you always enjoy how the sunlight shines
wonderfully through the clouds and how the fresh
breeze whispers after an afternoon rain.
May you always love the sound of children laughing
and the wet kisses of exuberant puppies.
I hope you find solace in the quiet peace of lazy
morning and the warmth of cozy nights by a
crackling fire.
May you always find your way home, and may your
burdens be always light.
I hope you fall in love with being alive and that you
remember every day
That you are amazing and that you're worthy of
lasting love.
May you always remember to take care of yourself

and that loving yourself is as important as loving your people.

I hope you fill your days with adventure and your nights with peace.

More than anything,

May hugs find you when you're down and smiles warm your heart when you need it most.

I hope that you always have comfort on difficult days and joy on your best days.

May you have the patience to see things through and hope enough to never stop believing.

On these days that lie ahead, may you always have the most beautiful happiness and the wisdom to understand the hardest lessons.

My wish for you,

Most of all, is to simply have love.

For yourself, for your people and for being alive.

The love to complete your life and always help you find your way.

These things, among so many wishes that I have for you,

Will always be in my heart as I think of you.

You're beautiful, you're special ...

You'll always be loved more than you'll ever know.

Now and for always.

She Says Nothing When She Wants to Say Everything

It's not her words that tell her story.
It's the quiet storms behind her eyes that protect her truths.
She may say very little sometimes because she says so much more with how she looks at you, the expressions of her soulful emotions.
Her quiet resolve and smoldering intensity belie the solemn battle that she often fights inside.
The worries,
The fears.
The insecurities and doubts that she faces every day.
She wonders if she's enough ...
If she is a good person and if people like her.
Things she knows she shouldn't care about ... but can't help the worry nonetheless.
Her mirror shows her every imperfection that plagues her confidence.
She just wants the simplest of things in the most complex ways:
To be loved, to feel worthy, to be appreciated and respected.
She fights battles that most never know about in ways they'll never understand.
Most of all,
She'll hide her silent angst beneath a happy smile and an upbeat laugh.
She'll cry quickly when no one is looking and wipe it

away just as swiftly.

Most will never know the hurt she buries just to be happy and find her joy.

She's strong, resilient and prideful – she doesn't want anyone's pity or judgement.

She's a mess more often than not, though most would never know.

She wants to be understood though she doesn't even understand herself sometimes.

She knows she can be a disaster, and she's okay with that.

She reminds herself often that she's strong, she's beautiful and she's going to find her way.

But if you ever look at her and wonder just who she is and what's she thinking,

start with everything she doesn't say.

After all, she says it best when she says nothing at all.

Every Time She Laughs

Why am I so madly in love with you?
It's so much more than your beauty or what you say,
more than your adorable smirk or the clever quips
you make.
I'm at a loss for words to describe the effect you
have on me ...
It's in the way you smile,
the twinkle in your eye and even in the way you
carry yourself.
Your charm, your personality, your heart and soul ...
There's so many reasons why I'm so enamored with
you that I'd like to spend the rest of my days
enjoying you.
Truth is, I've decided simply to embrace every day
and show you in countless ways the amazing
blessing you are to me ...
To appreciate the person you are and everything
you mean to me.
When you smiled, you had my attention.
When you talked, you captured my mind.
When you laughed, you stole my heart.
When you looked in my eyes, you won my love
forever.
I thought making you laugh would undoubtedly make
you fall for me,
but every time I hear that mischievous and beautiful
giggle, I can't help but fall in love with you all over
again.
Me and you,
Laughing, loving and living our best life ...

The essence of every dream I've ever had for what real love would truly be.

That's my promise and hope for every tomorrow.

Until then, I'll simply drink in the beautiful hue of your sparking eyes,

I'll smile at your joyful laughter,

And most of all,

I'll embrace you with every part of my heart, mind and soul.

Just know this:

You'll always find me waiting for you ... on the steps to forever,

Loving you, endlessly.

Where the Truth Lies

She was a woman like any other, yet completely
unique in the most quietly gorgeous ways.
Her strong spirit tucked away her mysteries behind
dark eyes, masking a soul brimming with wonder
and beauty … complete with emotions that seemed
never to waver.
Known by many, understood by few and loved by all,
she had a way about her that most just didn't get,
and she was okay with that.
She knew who she was and what she wanted.
They heard her words of reassurance and believed
her laugh because they never saw the anguish
hidden in her soul.
She was the one who could bury her pain behind a
smile, any discomfort through a joke, dismiss her
disappointment through a simple "it's okay."
Truth was, it never was … she never was.
She braved the world with a dazzling smile not
because she felt amazing, but because she was
strong.
No matter what she said or showed, she always
cared – about herself, her people and how others
saw her – because that's just who she was and how
she loved.
She couldn't simply write people off or stop caring,
regardless of how much they hurt her.
She didn't know how to love halfway or selfishly, and
though she had a magnanimous and beautiful heart,
it seemed to be constantly bleeding from the pain.
Her way had always been to love passionately, live

without regret and seek the answers to every question of her heart.

She vowed long ago to live unapologetically, and regardless of the why, she always sought the truth.

The only way she could keep the depths of her soul intact and beautiful was to tuck it away, hidden beneath the guise of a façade of placid contentment.

She kept her walls high – not to keep others out, but to see who cared enough to tear them down ...

Yet, the one person she longed for was the one who would see her for who she truly was and would accept her for every glorious imperfection and wonderful flaw.

That was her gift and curse, knowing without saying, loving without caution and caring when she shouldn't.

She paid the price many times over for what many would say is folly,

but she knew better – she wouldn't change who she was, regardless of how it hurt sometimes.

She would never accept halfway love and lackluster passion; she needed more than that.

She would follow her heart and often leave her head behind ...

Her heart would be shattered into countless pieces ... And yet, somehow, she still believed in love.

In her world, the only path to catching her dreams and finding true love was to follow her heart.

That's just who she was and how she lived her life. No apologies and no regrets.

She knew that one day she would stop wishing on shooting stars and instead,

Become one herself.
In a night full of lights, she was always meant to be shining beautifully,
And she knew that she would never look back and lament her broken roads.
The brightest diamonds are forged under the toughest pressure, and she was meant to be the most brilliant light –
In how she shined, how she sparkled ...
And most of all,
How she loved.

Love Itself Isn't Enough to Make Forever Possible

Most of us think happily ever after is just a story of
butterflies and happy times, and it is ...
But it's so much more than that.
It's a tale of devotion, respect, love and
communication.
I knew when I realized that I fell in love with you,
That was just the beginning.
The happiness and warm fuzzy feelings of love are
amazing,
But there's so much more.
Anyone can fall in love, but it takes work to stay in
love.
It requires loyalty and commitment,
passion and effort and never being lazy or selfish in
love.
Putting each other first, doing what's best for
ourselves and each other, and never forgetting the
love in our hearts.
Our relationship started with love,
was built with trust and respect,
And was strengthened by work and communication.
Sometimes, it's more than the big moments that take
our breaths away, but all the little ones as well.
Sometimes, saying "I'm sorry" isn't to admit fault,
But rather to express that the relationship is more
important than your ego.
I'll never lose my love and desire for you,
Our passion will always be kindled in your eyes.

I know that forever takes work ... every day.
I can't just tell you that I love you.
I have to show you.
Love and compassion through action and selfless virtue.
Romance and passion have their place,
But it's what we do when we face the world together that matters.
Hand in hand, we can overcome anything so long as we communicate,
Learn to compromise,
And understand each other's needs.
We will never be perfect,
Nor will our relationship.
But with hard work and lots of love,
We will always be perfect for each other.
So, let's make a promise to each other, here and now –
Let's always fall in love, all over again ...
Every ... single ... day.

I Am the Phoenix, Forged in Flames, Stronger for the Struggle

My story is a tale of failure and falling,
A time when I didn't know if I could ever find my strength again.
When you're on your knees trying to muster the courage to stand again, everything seems impossible.
Nothing is easy when you're down and out, and everywhere you turn, you find only disappointment.
From broken hearts to broken roads, it's easy to get lost in the battle for survival.
Moments turned into memories, and before I knew it, I was buried beneath the faded dreams of yesterday.
Truth is, though, it's in those moments when the fires of struggle threaten to tear your spirit apart that you make a choice.
Choose to lose yourself in the flames of misery or face the flames and become the fire ...
Rise again reborn, the phoenix from the ashes of a painful past.
Sometimes, you find your strength when being strong is the only option you have.
Forged in the flames of fiery trials, I refused to let my failures define me.
I knew that to survive, to become stronger and better, I had to transform my tragedy into triumph.
No excuses, settling or half efforts.
The best way to dig out of a hole is to do it with all your heart, filled with passion and motivated by pain.

I couldn't always see the light of better days, and there are still days that I want to quit,
But I know I'm better than that.
I deserve more than that.
This is my life and my choice, and I choose to live my life with relentless optimism and zealous courage.
I won't be reduced, defined or defeated by the people and past that tried to destroy me.
The fire burning in my heart can't be quenched, and I won't accept anything or anyone in my life who doesn't accept me for the brokenly beautiful person that I am.
I don't need anyone's pity, handout or sympathy ...
I just want their best, all the time in all the ways.
Love me or leave me, I'll always be respected and appreciated ...
On my terms, no more and no less.
Yes, my struggles scared and scarred me, but those are just the reminders of where I've been, not where I'm going.
I'm not who I was, and I'm not yet who I am meant to be, but that's the beauty of writing my own story:
I can create every chapter of my life just the way I want in the way I choose.
No matter where I go and what I do, whenever you meet me, you'll realize one thing about me.
I'll never be complacent, ordinary or lackluster ...
In all the ways that matter to all the people
who I care about –
Heart, spirit and soul ...
I'll always be on fire for being alive.

Kiss Her as if You Are Writing Poetry on Her Soul

Would your lips tremble if I kissed them?
Would your heart melt if I ignited your passion?
Would your soul long for mine if I called out for you?
Would your love be mine if I chose you, ever after?
As the hands of time edge tenuously forward,
I hold everything in my arms
As I look at you.
I don't know how I found you or why I am so
blessed,
only that I look at you daily and wonder how
Such a beautiful love could enrapture me.
So, as I take your soft face into my hands,
drinking in your soulful eyes,
I wonder so many things,
but most of all, this:
If I fall into the madness of your love,
plunge headfirst into the depths of your heart,
will you catch me and keep me, forevermore?
It's a chance I'm willing to take.

Please Just Hold My Hand

I know there are times when you look at me and just don't know how you can help me.
My emotions can get the best of me, and I can see that you feel helpless as you watch me struggle.
Know that I'll be okay, even if I'm sad for a time.
A lot of the time, I won't even know why I'm down, only that I am.
Luckily, I've long since learned my way through those times, and they don't last long.
Those are the moments I don't need you to try to solve my problems or conquer the world for me.
I just want you to be there for me,
To listen to me and let me vent.
I know you're used to being the one who fixes everything, but I don't need to be fixed and every problem doesn't have a solution ...
Those are the times you should try listen to my soul as it struggles.
Don't be sad for me as I work through my angst, I can handle it all as I always have ...
I'm just thankful you're by my side now.
Your hand in mine is all the reassurance I need to get past what's in my head ...
The worries, the fears, the insecurities.
Often, I just need time and compassion to work through the myriad of thoughts and emotions.
If you were to ask me why I feel down, I may not even know sometimes ...
But you being there makes all the difference to me, and I'm so grateful to not have to face it all alone

anymore.

So, as you watch the feelings wash across my face,
know that I'll find my way ...

I always do.

I know it's hard watching the one you love struggle,
but you're doing just what I need by being there,
supporting me and loving me.

I may not always be easy, I may not always make
sense ...

But rain or shine,

Our love will always be worth it in the end.

I Will Never Apologize for Who I Am

There comes a time when you realize that not
everyone is going to like you.
Sometimes, they dislike you for no reason, and
there's nothing you can do.
Whatever their motivations are – jealousy,
unhappiness or personal challenges – realize that
it's not you.
It's not really you that they dislike, but themselves.
You can't fix other people nor should you try to.
Empower yourself each and every day to be the best
you that you can be ...
that's all you can do, all you can control.
Stop and take a deep breath.
You're never going to be everyone's favorite person,
and trying to please everyone will lead to your
unhappiness.
Be real, be yourself and always be authentic.
Celebrate your uniqueness and invigorate your
passions.
It's better to be disliked for being genuine than to be
loved for being fake.
Love your people who accept and appreciate you ...
walk past the rest.
Life is full of people trying to be what they aren't to
get things they don't need to impress people that
don't matter.
You've got one life, make it count.
There is no dress rehearsal.
Do it your way, with your style and let your voice be
heard.

Who you are and what you do may not matter to everyone else, but it will always matter to those who love you.
If you are going to make ripples,
you might as well create waves.
You were born for greatness ...
Own it, love it and let your light shine.
This is your time –
Spread your wings.
Take the chance to fall in love with being alive, every day.
You don't ever have to apologize for being amazing ... It's your time to shine, my dear.
Live passionately, love intensely and always be unforgettably you.

Before You Assume …

Maybe you don't like me or understand me, but you
don't have to – I don't need your approval to be
happy in my way.
I shine in my own light, love it or leave it.
Just because you don't understand me doesn't mean
I don't care.
I may not always be bubbly and smiling,
but it doesn't mean I don't love life like you do.
The things you don't know about me don't give you
the right to assume or judge me.
I have my own style and way of doing things, and
perhaps that's not your way … but it doesn't make
either of us wrong.
Don't assume you know me when you've never even
taken the time to speak to me … understand me …
or even befriend me.
Yeah, I smile and maybe flirt a little,
but that doesn't mean I'm easy to fall in love.
I'm blunt and to the point, but that doesn't mean I'm
hurtful.
There are times that I just prefer to be alone,
thinking and reflecting …
It doesn't mean I don't like having friends or being
social.
I may wear my heart on my sleeve, but it doesn't
mean I'm naive or foolish.
Don't think I'm upset or sad because I'm quiet –
sometimes, I just want to be left alone, comfortable
in my solitude and introspection.
Often, it's just because I'm just sitting back and

observing the world around me.

That doesn't mean I'm shy or introverted.

So, please, do both of us a favor ...

Stop assuming and stop judging.

If you want answers, then you ask your questions.

If you prefer to stand back and make false assumptions, then do it somewhere else.

I don't have the time nor concern to try to prove myself to anyone,

Nor do I care to be judged by someone who doesn't know me.

I'm comfortable in my own skin, and that's what matters most.

I love me for me ... and I don't need approval for that.

Before you tell me to check my attitude, I wanted to let you know that I already have –

My attitude is great, and so is my life.

I'm not defined by where I've been or what I've done, but where I'm going and the kindness with which I treat others.

I am who I choose to be, and that's how I live, love and chase my dreams.

I expect everything and accept nothing less than the best.

Can you handle that?

Don't answer unless you want to listen to me as well.

I will never judge nor assume.

Can you say the same?

A Strong Cup of Coffee in a World Enamored with Cheap Wine

I'm more than an ordinary person with an average heart, I'm a wildfire fully alive.
I'm done chasing people who don't know what they want or who they are.
I'm going to be the one who lives fully in the moment, unapologetically.
I may not always be the best at making plans, and I may forget where I'm going some days, but I'll always be real.
I'll tell it like it is and speak from my heart – probably even when I shouldn't, sometimes.
I don't sugarcoat my personality, and I don't make things up to comfort myself.
I'm authentic, I'm genuine and I'm always down to earth.
I don't apologize for speaking my truths, and I'll never comfort you with a lie –
We both deserve better than that.
So, give me the people who seek the light, who feel life with their souls and follow their hearts.
Save the lukewarm passion and mediocre love for weak coffee and stale leftovers.
I'm going to keep my circle small and the walls around my heart high.
I expect what I give, and I always give my all ...
Whether it's life, love or just spending time together, I'll always be there, present in the moment.
If you want to win my heart, start with knowing your

own.

I don't need anyone with uncertain dreams and iffy loyalty in my life or love.

I can't hold your hand through the storms if you don't know where you stand when it starts raining.

I need your best, each and every day, because that's what I give.

I'll be chasing dreams, lying under starlit night skies and losing my thoughts somewhere on a windswept beach ...

So, if you're not all in, with passion and soulful love, then leave me be.

Yes, I'm a dreamer, but I'm not the only one.

Yes, I'm a lover, but I know the love I deserve.

Yes, I'm a fighter but I'll never settle.

Forget the shallow love and superficial needs, I'll always be the one who needs much more than that.

Give me the deep talks for hours.

Share your wildest dreams and most vibrant desires.

Most of all, bare your soul with vulnerability and visceral honesty.

Some would say that I expect too much, but that's their loss.

I'll never live with regret or love with apology.

In a world full of the same roses,

I'll always choose to be a unique wildflower.

The Priority

If you want to write a beautiful love story, start with the things that matter most:
Love, respect, passion, honesty.
But that, my friends, just begins your tale.
Falling in love happens every day, all around us ...
Love yourself first and let the love of others follow.
It's wonderful, captivating and will take your breath away.
But if you want a real and lasting relationship, the kind that transcends challenges and hard times,
You must be willing to do what it takes to fall in love ... every single day.
If you want a love story, then take the time to write quality chapters.
Put in the work, be thoughtful and make her a priority.
Communicate your hopes, dreams and desires.
If you want to share a life with someone, then share your heart openly and freely.
They fell in love with you –
Share your heart, mind and soul to remind them why ... often.
Don't be afraid to expose your vulnerabilities, for the right person will love you even more for doing so.
Make respect and appreciation priorities for your relationship.
Their time, their needs and their heart should always be valued.
If you want to be treated with respect, then carry yourself with dignity.

Character breeds class.

Don't be lazy in love.

Write her a love note.

Surprise her with ice cream.

Plan a date.

Cook him breakfast in bed.

Have pride ...

In yourself, your partner and your relationship.

Make them feel special by being proud of your love.

In the end, choose to have an unforgettable love story.

Every fairy tale starts with two hearts that found each other against all odds.

It's up to you to bring your own magic.

I'm also here to tell you ...

You're never too old to believe in magic ...

And the most beautiful love will always be just that: Magical.

Choose to make your story the most magical of all.

So Much More

As much as I wanted to know,
I never understood why things never worked out the way I wanted.
No matter who I loved or what I wanted, no amount of hoping seemed to bring me happiness ...
Doors closed and my heart broke so many times that I started to wonder if I'd ever find love and happiness.
It's easy to fall into despair and think that you'll end up alone sometimes.
Not because I wanted to, but because everything I always hoped for seemed to inevitably go wrong.
People would tell me to "hang in there" and "it'll happen for you," but I started to believe that their words of comfort were just what people were supposed to say.
I crashed so many times in my journey that I didn't know if I'd ever find the crossroads to happiness.
Continuing to believe in love when your heart has been broken is seemingly an impossible task, and one that I failed repeatedly on so many days.
Sometimes, it seemed easier to wallow in misery and ask "why me?"
Than to dust yourself off and pick yourself up.
"Meant to be" seems like a fairy tale read to children ... Until it happens to you.
When I stopped focusing on chasing the ones who didn't want to be caught and started learning how to love myself, things began to change.
It wasn't easy, and there are still many days when I

feel like giving up, but I know that at the end of the day, I'll always be more than okay … I'll be happy. Happy with myself, happy with my life, happy with my choices.

I finally realized that before, when I was willing to settle for "good enough," was when and why things never worked out –

Because I deserved so much more.

Rain or shine, rise or fail, I'll choose to be happy on my terms, in my way, for myself.

So, if "meant to be" finds me when the time is right, then I'll be ecstatic ... with open arms and a willing heart.

Until then, I'll keep loving my life, living my truth and always seeking the sunlight.

Who Am I? That's a Secret

She's a mystery hidden behind a pretty smile, an
enigma lying behind her soulful eyes.
Just waiting for the right person to come along and
unravel her secrets.
Her smile is full of magic and her laughter echoes of
pure passion.
She makes her mark upon whomever she touches
and leaves everyone wondering ...
Who was that loving soul that just crossed my path?
Her eyes hide the depths of her hidden soul,
protected by the walls she's cultivated for many
years.
She doesn't hide from the world, but, in fact,
Embraces life with a vivacious zeal that can't be
duplicated.
She'll leave you breathless and amazed with the
hope that she weaves with her spirit,
The happiness that she inspires with her words.
Some would almost say she's not real –
Here one minute, gone the next,
Fleeting as the wind as she chases her dreams.
But, if you ever do happen upon this beautiful soul
that sings of perfect imperfection,
Just stop and take in the serenity of those moments
... Because like the wind, she'll be gone in an instant
... And you'll wonder what magical creature you
discovered ...
But then you'll realize the truth:
She's the consummate woman in search of love,
And that's a wonder to behold.

If you dare to catch this mythical butterfly,
Make love to her mind,
Romance her soul
And kindle her passions.
Try to dive deeply into the rich windows to her soul,
and discover the truth of who she really is.
So, when you find her standing in front of you,
Embrace all of her with your entirety,
For a woman like her comes along,
But once in a lifetime.
Don't let her slip out of your grasp wondering how
you ever let her get away.

Sometimes She Needs You to Just Be There

I know that you've been bruised, broken and
battered.
I see the pain in your eyes.
I know I can't make it go away or always make it
better.
You don't always need me to rescue you, fight for
you or save the day.
Sometimes, you just need me ...
To be there and care.
Sometimes, listening is all you want.
Not to offer you a solution or try to fix everything, but
just to rest your weary soul on my shoulder.
I'll give you refuge on those days – when the world
has just been too much and has worn you down.
Know that I'll always love you for the woman that
you are and the soulful spirit you've always been.
I don't have all the answers, but then, you don't
need me to.
Sometimes, all you need is just me ...
To hold you, to listen, to care.
I'll always be there for the laughter, the tears and
everything in between.
Together, there's nothing we can't overcome.
In the meantime, just hold my hand and I'll protect
your heart.
There's nothing stronger than our love.
I'll stand with you through the storms and dance with

you in the rain.
Me and you, forever.

A Hug to Heal Your Broken Pieces

There will be much in this world to dim your smile,
Many things that will cause you pain,
But there is also much more that is worthwhile,
To brighten your smile and fill your heart.

Somewhere, someone is searching for you,
Scarred, bent and broken as we all are,
Know that your love is meant to be true,
For your many nights of wishing on a star isn't in
vain.

Those nights of loneliness and sighs of ache
Will soon be a distant memory upon which
You will finally believe in love, yours to have
As you hold them close, feelings so rich.

This is the dream and promise of the lonely hearted,
One that will be blessed if you don't lose faith,
The journey to find love that you long ago started,
The true love, yours forever until the sun's fading
rays.

You'll never know the when or how of love –
What's meant to be has its own time,
Just know that love is meant for us all,
Be open to love and embrace your heart
When love finally comes calling.

That's when you'll grasp the promise of us –
The love we've been destined for,

Finally arriving as we have longed for ...
I've always been waiting past the horizon for you ...

My love, my soulmate,
My one true thing.
Always and forever,
Love everlasting.

I'm Not Like the Others. That Was Your First Mistake

I think it's time we got a few things straight.
If you want just another lover or average relationship, then I'm not the one for you.
Maybe you're not used to a person who speaks their mind and means what they say, but I'm all of the above.
I have a voice, and I will always be heard, even if you don't like what I have to say.
That doesn't mean I won't listen, it just means that I expect equality.
Don't walk in front of me, I won't follow.
Don't walk behind me, I don't want to lead.
Just walk beside me and hold my hand.
No, I don't want to hear the stories of who you used to date or your past love affairs.
I will always appreciate where you've been and who you've fought to become, I just don't need to hear about past loves.
I'm more focused on building a future together than I am hearing why they ever broke your heart.
We all have baggage, and I'll help you unpack, but things we should share constantly aren't exes and lost loves.
We should be building a future with communication, respect, passion and love ...
Not the broken hearts of yesteryear.
Let's work to tell our story, together, and stop sharing the narrative of the people we've let go.

Some people were meant to be in our hearts, not our lives ...
Or in the stories we tell.
There's a reason why they're in the past, so let's leave them there.
I'll never ask you to forget the people who once walked with you on your journey, I just don't want to hear all about the ones that got away.
I'll never be passive or be a doormat.
I don't care why they are gone or what they liked, I care about where you and I are going.
We can't build a future if you're stuck in the past.
So, if you want someone like all the others, then you should look elsewhere.
If you're willing to commit to a healthy and happy love story, then let's start writing our chapters for us, not everyone else.
We can't look forward if we're looking over our shoulders at the past.
Today, me and you, and where we're headed ... that's what matters ...
Not staying wrapped up in the places and people that broke our hearts.
Let's share our stories and move on to building a future, together.
Can you roll with that?

I Never Blamed You ... I Only Blamed Me for Making You My Everything

When I think about what happened to us, it just makes me sad.
Not because of what you did, but because of what I let myself become ...
I stopped being myself and started trying to be something I wasn't ... to make you happy.
I lost myself in us so much that there wasn't a "me" anymore –
At least not the person that I used to be.
That's not your fault, it's mine.
You didn't ask me to change but part of you hoped I would become what you wanted.
You thought you would be happy if I changed ...
And it still wasn't enough to save us.
We lost our way and learned that sometimes, love alone just isn't enough.
I don't know all the reasons why we didn't work,
Only that I never should have pinned all my hopes and happiness on you.
That wasn't fair to you, and it never gave us a chance.
I thought I was doing what you wanted, being what you needed to be happy ...
But I was wrong.
Who I became and what happened made both of us lose faith in ourselves and each other.
I've found the strength to forgive you for walking away,

But more than that, I uncovered the courage to forgive myself.

Most of all,

I should thank you for setting me free to make my way back to start my journey of self-discovery.

I was so lost for so long because I depended on you to make me happy, and when you left, I didn't think I would be ever be whole again.

So many days, I didn't even want to get out of bed, because wallowing in misery seemed so much easier than digging myself out of the sadness.

That's when something clicked in me, and I realized I needed to remember who I was ...

Before you, before us, before the heartbreak.

Strong, beautiful and vibrant, I was once a wonderful soul who loved my life.

The path back to myself hasn't been easy, and there's been days I wanted to quit, but I found my way, somehow.

I'll never forget us and the times we had, it'll always have a special place in my heart,

But it no longer defines me and it no longer hurts ...

That's how I know I've healed and made peace with all that happened.

Thank you for showing me the way back home to myself.

I know now that I'm loved, I'm special and I'm worthy ... Of all the love in the world.

I finally remembered how to love myself the way I should have all along.

Everything You'll Never Understand

She was restless in ways she couldn't explain,
Deeply in her soul ...
Buried in places that she didn't always understand.
She built walls, not to keep everyone out,
But to see who cared enough to try to tear them down.
Everyone knew her,
But no one really did.
Always smiling, always laughing,
She was a friend to all and seemed so happy ...
But then, no one ever really knew the pain behind her eyes.
In places that the others couldn't see,
Understand or even begin to know.
She yearned to share her soul with someone who understood her for who she was.
She cried often in the twilight,
Alone and disconsolate ...
Wanting nothing more than peace,
If only for a time.
She didn't need or ask for anything,
Because she was like the strongest wind,
Unbreakable and unmistakable.
But she yearned for more.
Just the one chance, that one opportunity to come out from behind the mask.
She'd love and live with no regrets, and that's who she was.
She carried a light in her heart and a glow in her soul,

And she knew that someday, someone would see that beacon and find their way home to her arms.
Until then, she'd embrace her darkness, make love to her light and laugh through the tears.
Because she was a lioness, and that's what queens do.
Then one day … there was a wolf.
Not diabolical, dark or brooding,
But the quintessential gentleman wolf.
That's when she finally realized …
Even a queen needs her king.
Sometimes, the stories with the saddest beginnings have the happiest endings.
She never needed to be completed, found or made happy … she was content with her life just the way she liked it –
Fierce, independent and free …
Until him.
He made her understand that happiness is best when shared with others.
He appreciated, accepted and respected her.
Most of all, he just loved her and showed her it was okay to tear down her walls and
Build a future with him.
So … that's what she did,
And never looked back.
One beautiful day at a time.

My Story Has Yet to Be Written

It's okay to start my new story today.
Those mistakes I've made along the way aren't
failures, they're lessons.
I've stumbled and fallen more times than I can
count, yet I'm still standing ...
I'll not stop dreaming of where I am going to go.
I'll never be defined by my disappointments; I'm
forged by the fires of what I've overcome.
I'm more than a survivor,
Much more than a dreamer.
I'm an achiever.
Reinventing myself doesn't have an expiration, and
dreams don't have deadlines.
Yes, I've had a rough time lately, and some days I
don't even want to get out of bed.
Those are the times that I take a deep breath and
remember that I have purpose,
That I'm meant for more than where I've been.
I don't have it all figured out; in fact, I don't always
see the next step ahead.
But that's okay, I don't have to know my whole story
or even the next chapter,
As long as I pick up the pen and start writing.
I'm a beautiful, unique and strong soul growing
through this journey called life.
That's the thing about journeys, you don't have to
know the whole story or even the destination, so
long as you keep moving forward.
I know there's going to be rough days and hard
weeks, but I can handle anything because I know

that my future self is cheering me on every step of the way.

I know that no matter what, I'll get there, where I'm meant to go.

I'll fight for my dreams with fiery passion and a hardy spirit, because I refuse to settle for less than I deserve ...

And that's what is most important –

Always remembering that I'm worth it.

I'll never listen to the doubters and nonbelievers because they're not walking my path,

They don't know the person that I am.

That's just the thing – they don't have to.

I'm fierce, I'm bold, and I won't be denied what I know I deserve.

This is my story and my dream.

I'm writing a new chapter in my life, turning my setbacks into a comeback ...

With fire in my heart and love in my soul,

I'll always find my way.